# KID UNDER COVER

Lead chewed up the ground behind Clint as he carried the boy from the line of fire, pushing him into a drywash and diving in on top of him. He drew his gun and waited.

Once they had gained cover, the firing stopped and it got quiet. Clint felt a sting in his left leg and looked down to see a wet, red patch on his calf. Then the pain set it.

"Clint?" Billy said, his voice muffled because his face was in the ground.

"Yes, Billy?"

Billy lifted his head and asked, "Am I shot?"

"No, partner, you're not shot."

"Are you shot?"

Clint gritted his teeth as the pain from the bullet wound flashed up his leg and said, "Oh, yeah."

## DON'T MISS THESE ALL-ACTION WESTERN SERIES FROM THE BERKLEY PUBLISHING GROUP

J. R. ROBERTS

JOVE BOOKS, NEW YORK

BULLETS FOR A BOY

A Jove Book / published by arrangement with
the author

PRINTING HISTORY
Jove edition / April 2001


For information address: The Berkley Publishing Group,
a division of Penguin Putnam Inc.,
375 Hudson Street, New York, New York 10014.

The Penguin Putnam Inc. World Wide Web site address is
http://www.penguinputnam.com

ISBN: 0-515-13047-8

A JOVE BOOK®
Jove Books are published by The Berkley Publishing Group,
a division of Penguin Putnam Inc.,
375 Hudson Street, New York, New York 10014.
JOVE and the "J" design
are trademarks belonging to Penguin Putnam Inc.

PRINTED IN THE UNITED STATES OF AMERICA

10 9 8 7 6 5 4 3 2 1

THE
GUNSMITH
232
BULLETS FOR A BOY

# ONE

Clint saw the walking figure from far off and didn't realize at first what it was. A person, certainly, on foot in the middle of nowhere, but he couldn't make out whether it was a man or a woman. When he finally realized it was a child he felt foolish and quickened his horse's pace.

When he reached the child he saw that it was a boy, no more than four or five. He was dirty, his shirt was torn, but he wasn't crying, and he had a look of quiet determination on his face.

Clint dismounted and crouched in front of the boy.

"Hold on there, son," he said.

The boy had been looking at the ground and now lifted his eyes to look at Clint. They were blue, as blue as he'd ever seen and, at the moment, totally devoid of emotion. Immediately he knew that the boy was in shock.

Clint took hold of the boy by the shoulders and checked him for injuries. He had a cut on his cheek and a scraped chin, but there didn't seem to be any serious injuries.

"Son, are you all right?"

The boy seemed to consider the question for a moment, then simply nodded his head.

"Can you talk?"

Again he thought it over, then simply shrugged.

"Where are your parents?"

In answer to that question, he simply turned and pointed behind him.

"Back there?"

The boy nodded. He wondered how far the boy could have walked.

"Are you thirsty?"

The boy didn't have to think that over. He nodded vigorously. Clint got his canteen from his saddle and gave it to the boy. The boy gulped down some water and Clint was about to stop him when he stopped on his own and handed the canteen back. Clint hung it back on the saddle.

"Why don't you come for a ride with me?" Clint said to the boy, who nodded.

Clint lifted the child and placed him on the saddle, then mounted up behind him.

"Let's see if we can find your parents," Clint said.

The boy didn't say anything. He just sat there rubbing Eclipse's neck over and over again.

"Okay," Clint said, "that's okay. We'll just go and find them."

He was surprised at how far they had ridden before they finally found the boy's parents. They found an overturned Conestoga wagon, the contents of which had been strewn about. He didn't know if that was a result of the wagon turning over or if someone had gone inside and tossed the stuff out.

He dismounted and said to the boy, "You stay right there, and I'll have a look around."

The boy didn't answer. He was still patting Eclipse's neck.

Clint walked over to the wagon, stepping around the debris that seemed to be made up of personal items. There was clothing and bits of furniture, what looked like curtains, and some pots and pans. On the other side of the wagon he found a chest of drawers which had been smashed and the contents scattered about.

He found the woman inside the wagon. She was lying on her back, staring up at him sightlessly. Her dress had been hiked up around her waist and there was blood between her legs. It was obvious she had been raped, and that whoever had done it had shot her in the chest. Or maybe they'd shot and killed her and then raped her, depending on how depraved they were.

For a few moments he thought that perhaps whoever had done this had taken the man with them, but then he found his body pinned beneath the wagon. Having the wagon fall on him hadn't killed him, though, as he also had a bullet in his head. Clint wondered if the man had lived long enough to hear his wife screaming.

And then there was the boy. He turned and saw the child still sitting astride Eclipse. There were no other children around, but that didn't mean there hadn't been any. If this had been done by Indians, or *comancheros*, they might have taken another child with them. Although Indians probably would have taken a boy this young to raise among them. A female child would have been taken for another reason entirely.

He walked back to the boy and looked up at him.

"Son?"

The boy didn't answer or look at him.

"Do you have any brothers or sisters?"

Still the boy didn't answer. Clint reached up and touched his shoulder.

"It's all right," Clint said. "Nothing is going to happen to you. But I need to know if you have any brothers or sisters I should be looking for."

The boy looked at him, then said softly, "No."

Clint looked surprised. He'd expected a simple nod or a shake of the head.

"You can talk?"

"Yes, sir."

"Why haven't you talked to me before this?"

The boy took a deep breath, as if he was about to impart some pearl of great wisdom, and said, "I'm not supposed to talk to strangers, sir."

"Well," Clint said, not knowing exactly *what* to say to that, "well, my name is Clint. What's yours?"

"Billy."

"Okay, Billy," Clint said, "now we know each other's names so we're not strangers anymore, are we?"

"No, sir."

Clint looked around. The nearest place he knew of that would have a lawman, and someone to watch after the child, was Denver. He'd have to bypass several smaller towns to get to it, but he didn't think they'd have the facilities to deal with this anyway. What he could do, however, was stop in one of them if it had a telegraph office and send a message on ahead so they'd be ready for him when he arrived with the boy.

"All right, Billy," Clint said, "we're going to go and find someone to help us take care of your parents, all right?"

"Yes, sir."

Clint mounted up again, turned Eclipse and, with one last look at the carnage that was left of what was once Billy's life, headed for the nearest town.

# TWO

The next town was called Littleton, and Clint was happy to see the telegraph wires as he rode up to it. He passed the livery because, if things went well, he had no intention of staying in town any longer than it took to send the telegram and feed the boy. There was still plenty of daylight left to get closer to Denver so they could be there tomorrow.

His first stop was the sheriff's office. The man with the badge looked up from his desk as they entered and eyed Clint and the boy curiously.

"Help ya?" he asked. He had the biggest gray mustache Clint had ever seen; it hid his entire mouth from view. It looked as if he were speaking without moving it.

"Sheriff, I found this boy a few miles south of here," Clint said. He considered lowering his voice, but the boy would hear him even if he did. Also, it didn't much matter if he heard or not because he certainly knew what had happened. "He was traveling in a wagon with his parents."

"And where are they?"

"They're dead," Clint said. "They were killed, and I found the boy wandering on foot."

The sheriff looked at the boy and said, "Poor kid. What's his name?"

"It's Billy."

"Billy what?"

"I don't know that," Clint said. He looked down at the boy, who was holding his hand tightly and trembling. Clint crouched down. "Billy, you can relax. This man is the sheriff. He's one of the good guys. Understand?"

"Yes, sir."

"Do you know your last name?"

"Yes, sir."

"Can you tell us?"

"Hicks," the boy said.

Clint looked at the sheriff.

"That ring a bell with you, Sheriff?"

"I don't know no family named Hicks hereabouts," the lawman said.

"Well, it looked to me like they were coming from the east," Clint said. "They were both shot and the woman was . . . used."

The sheriff understood and looked immediately at Billy Hicks, who did not react.

"That's a damn shame," the sheriff said. "I'll get somebody out there to recover the bodies. What are you gonna do with the boy?"

"Well, unless you can provide for him here I'll take him to Denver with me," Clint said.

"No," the man said, "we got no way to take care of him here. I got a wife, but we're gettin' on a might to have a little tyke around."

The sheriff didn't look much older than Clint, but he knew what the man meant.

"Denver's bound to have some homes for wayward or orphaned kids," the sheriff went on.

"I'm sure they will," Clint said. "Sheriff, I didn't go through the wagon, so if you manage to find a name and address of a relative we might be able to contact back east—maybe a letter or something—I'd be obliged if you'd send me a telegram in Denver at the Denver House hotel."

"Sure thing," the lawman said. "What's your name?"

"Clint Adams."

The sheriff froze as he reached for a pencil.

"The Gunsmith?"

"That's right."

The man grabbed the pencil and wrote the name of the hotel on the slip of paper.

"Yes, sir," he said. "I'll be glad to send you a telegram soon as I know something, Mr. Adams."

"Thanks. I'm going to send a telegram to Denver and then get the boy something to eat before we get back on the trail. Shouldn't take more than a couple of hours."

"Sure thing," the sheriff said. "My name's Tyler, by the way, Dave Tyler."

"Good to meet you," Clint said, shaking the man's hand. "Come on, Billy. You must be starving. I know I am."

"Yes, *sir*!" the boy said, with the first hint of animation since Clint had picked him up. The resiliency of children always amazed him.

# THREE

After leaving the sheriff's office, Clint changed the order he'd intended to do things. He decided to feed the boy first and then send the telegram. He found a small café and took Billy inside. The place was empty as it was between meals, and the motherly waitress took to the little boy right away.

"How you doin', sweetie?" she asked, bending over.

Billy didn't answer.

"You hungry?" she asked.

He nodded vigorously.

"How about some nice beef stew?"

Another nod.

"He's a cutie," she said to Clint. "He yours?"

"No," Clint said, "I'm just . . . taking care of him for a while. If it's all right with you we'll have two of those beef stews."

"Comin' up," she said with a smile. "I know two hungry men when I see 'em."

When she left, Billy leaned forward and said in a whisper, "I'm not a hungry man, I'm a hungry boy."

Clint whispered back, "I think she knows that, Billy. She's just trying to be nice."

Billy sat back.

The waitress returned with a pot of coffee for Clint and a big glass of milk for Billy.

"Thought you fellas might be thirsty," she said, standing there with the tray for a moment, frowning. "Now, who'd like the milk?"

Billy looked at Clint, who nodded.

"I would!"

"Okay," she said, "the milk is yours, and the coffee will be for your . . . uncle?"

"His name's Clint," Billy said, after donning a milk mustache. "He's my friend."

"Your friend?" The waitress was clearly curious about the relationship between the two.

"My parents are dead, and he's helpin' me."

The waitress looked to Clint for confirmation, and he nodded.

"Just outside of town," he added.

"Oh, you poor boy," she said. "Does the sheriff know?" she asked Clint.

"We just came from there. He's arranging to have them . . . brought in."

"Indians?" she asked.

"I don't know," Clint said. "I guess we'll just have to wait and see."

She put her hand on Billy's head and said, "You're a very brave little boy."

When she left, Clint noticed that Billy looked very pensive.

"Billy?"

"I'm not, you know."

"Not what?"

Billy wouldn't meet his eyes.

"I'm not brave."

"Why do you say that?"

"Because I ran and hid," he said. "When those men came—"

"What men, Billy?"

Suddenly, he didn't seem to want to talk about that.

"Why did you hide, Billy?"

"Mama told me to."

"Did you always do what your mama told you?"

He hesitated, then said, "I tried."

"Then all you did was obey her, right?"

"Yes, sir."

"Then you did the right thing, Billy," Clint said. "Don't you worry about that anymore, okay?"

"Okay."

At this point the waitress appeared with their beef stew, and they both stopped talking and started eating.

Clint finished eating first. Billy was no less hungry, but he took smaller bites and was taking longer. When the sheriff appeared at the door of the café, Clint waved him off.

"Billy, I'll be right over by the door talking to the sheriff, okay?" he said to the boy.

Billy turned, saw the sheriff, then looked at Clint and said, "Okay, Clint."

Clint smiled and walked over to the sheriff.

"I've got a couple of men goin' out to pick up the boy's parents with a buckboard. What should we do with them?"

"Bury them, I guess," Clint said. "He's too small to

worry about that, I think. Just bury them, with their names if you can find them."

"We can ask the boy their names."

"He's liable to say Mama and Poppa, or something like that," Clint said, "but I'm not going to ask him now, if that's all right with you."

"If you don't mind, Mr. Adams," the sheriff said, "I think you and the boy should stay the night in the hotel until we get this straightened out."

Clint thought a moment, then said, "All right, Sheriff. I'll get a room, and then send the telegram to Denver. We'll leave in the morning. That suit you?"

"Yeah," the sheriff said, "that suits me fine."

"Thanks."

The sheriff nodded and left. Clint returned to the table in time to see Billy put away the last bite of stew. The waitress reappeared as if by magic and asked, "Who's ready for pie?"

# FOUR

Clint paid the bill while Billy tried to wipe the blueberry stains off his mouth with a napkin. Clint had had peach pie, his favorite, and it was some of the best he'd ever had.

"You stayin' in town?" the waitress asked him.

"Just overnight," Clint said. "Then I'm taking the boy to Denver where he can get some good care."

"You care about him, don't you?"

"Why wouldn't I?" he asked. "He's a little boy; wandering around out there helpless. Who wouldn't care?"

"A lot of men," she said, with a faraway look in her eyes, "a lot of men don't care about their own kids, let alone somebody else's." She refocused her eyes then and looked at him. "I'm thinkin' you must be some special kind of man."

"Doesn't take a special man to care for a child," he said.

"Well," she said, "where were you thinkin' of spendin' the night?"

"The hotel, I guess," he said. "This town does have a hotel, doesn't it?"

"If you can call it that," she said, "but a little boy doesn't belong there."

"What's wrong with it?"

"The beds are hard, and I'm sure it hasn't been cleaned in months," she said.

"Well, is there somewhere else?"

"There sure is," she said. "My place."

"Your—I couldn't ask you to do—"

"You ain't askin' me," she said, "I'm offerin'—for both of you. I got a house north of town. You can't miss it. It's painted yellow. I got extra rooms with soft beds." She crouched down next to Billy. "You'd like to sleep in a soft bed, wouldn't you, honey?" She touched his hair gently.

"Yes, ma'am, I would," he said. "I'm pretty tired."

"Yeah, you look tired," she said, and then stood and said to Clint, "and so do you. You take the boy to my house and stay there. I'll be home after I close up here, and I'll make some dinner."

"Miss—"

"Sandy," she said, "my name is Sandy."

"I'm Clint."

They shook hands.

"I'm Billy," Billy said, and held his hand out to her.

The sight of him with his hand out just about broke her heart.

"I don't shake hands with little boys," she said.

"Whataya do, then?" he asked, frowning.

"I kiss 'em!" she said, and quickly grabbed him and kissed his cheek.

"Yuck!" he said, wiping it off. "Kissin'!"

"You won't complain about having a pretty woman kiss you when you get a little older, Billy."

"Kissin'!" he said again, with disgust.

"Do we need a key to the house?" he asked her.

"No, it's open," she said. "We don't lock doors in this town. Everybody knows everybody."

"Sandy," he said, "I can't tell you how much I appreciate—"

"Forget it," she said. "I want Billy to have a good night's sleep, is all."

She crouched down again and said, "I'll see you later at my house, Billy."

"You ain't a-gonna kiss me again, are ya?" he asked, fearfully.

"No," she said, "I'm not going to kiss you again—not if you don't want me to."

"You can kiss Clint," Billy said.

"Well," she said, straightening up, "I'll keep that in mind."

Suddenly, Sandy didn't look like such a motherly type. Her black hair had some streaks of gray in it, and her face had some character lines, but she was an attractive woman, with a full, womanly body sheathed in a simple, cotton dress. Clint figured that she was probably a few years over forty, but wearing it well.

"Okay, Billy," he said, "let's go. We got one more stop to make, and then we'll go and get some rest."

Billy got down from his seat, his lips still bearing a trace of blueberry.

"Wash his face when you get to my house," she called after them as they went out. "There's plenty of soap."

"Soap!" Billy said, with the same tone in his voice he had used for *kissin'*.

Clint took Billy with him to the telegraph office, where he sent a telegram to Denver to his friend Talbot Roper, the private investigator. He figured Roper would know about some kind of a home that would take the boy in when they got there.

As they left the telegraph office, Billy said, "Are we gonna go get some sleep now?"

"Yep, Billy," Clint said, "that's exactly what we're going to go and do now."

# FIVE

Sandy's house did indeed have extra bedrooms—two of them. Clint got Billy bedded down in one of them and then roamed the house. He was tired, but not sleepy, and it wasn't even dark out, yet. He took a good look around and the only room he didn't go into was her bedroom. He figured the rest was fair game. He decided that she had been married at one time, but her husband had either died or left. There was just enough of a man left in the house to indicate that, otherwise it was warm and comfortable and definitely lived in and decorated by a woman.

There was a knock at the door a couple of hours after Billy fell asleep. Clint was sitting on the couch and the knock brought him out of a state of half-sleep. They had made one more stop after the telegraph office, and that was to tell the sheriff where they'd be staying. Clint went to the door and saw the lawman through the glass.

"Hello, Sheriff," he said, opening the door.

"Mr. Adams," Sheriff Tyler said. "How's the boy doin'?"

"He's asleep," Clint said. "Couple of hours now. Poor little guy was tuckered out."

"Can't blame him," Tyler said. "Wanted to let you know we brought in his parents and some of their belongings."

"Anything of value?"

"Not that we could see."

"Whoever killed them must've taken anything of value."

"Has the boy said anything about who it was?"

"Not a word," Clint said, "but he's starting to talk more and more. Eventually, he might say."

"Maybe in Denver," Tyler said.

"If they find out anything I'm sure they'll send you a telegram about it."

"I suppose," Tyler said. "I'm just hopin' it wasn't anybody from around here."

"Maybe somebody spotted them a ways back and followed them until they found a likely spot to hit them."

"Did you take a look at the ground?"

"It was pretty much trampled," Clint said. "I didn't take a real good look, but then it might not have mattered. I'm not the world's greatest tracker."

"Neither are the men I sent out there."

"Also, I was more concerned about the boy."

"Well, all right," Tyler said. "The bodies are at the undertaker's place. He'll get them ready to bury."

"Let me know how much it will be," Clint said.

"I think the town can foot the bill for the boy," Tyler said.

"That's real nice of you, Sheriff."

"Well," Tyler said, "least you'll eat good food stayin' here with Sandy."

"She said she'd be home after she closes," Clint said. "Any idea when that'll be?"

"Probably around eight," Tyler said. "Not a lot of people looking for dinner around here after that."

"Okay, thanks," Clint said. "I guess I'll just have to find some way to amuse myself until then."

"I'll probably be in the saloon later tonight," Tyler said. "Buy you a drink then?"

"Sure," Clint said. "See you there."

The sheriff nodded, turned, and stepped down off the porch. Clint closed the door and returned to the living room. Neither of them saw the man standing across the way watching them.

After Sheriff Tyler left the house, Willy Silver stepped from his hiding place and headed back toward town himself. He stayed far enough behind the sheriff so that he wouldn't be spotted, but could still keep the man in view. Once the sheriff went into his office Willy headed for the saloon, where he was supposed to meet up with Steve Harker.

In the saloon, Steve Harker was thinking how he had never killed a kid before, but it might have to be done this time. He wondered if he could get one of the others—Willy, or maybe Dale—to do it. After all, the boy was as much a threat to them as he was to Harker.

Seated at a table with a beer in front of him, he looked up just as Willy Silver came through the bat-wing doors. He went to the bar, got himself a beer, then took it over to the table where Harker was sitting and joined him.

"Well?"

"Adams and the boy are at the waitress's house."

"The waitress—you mean Sandy? From the café?"

"That's right."

"What are they doin' there?"

"I don't know," Harker said. "I just followed them there."

"That boy can identify us, Willy," Harker said.

"Only if he sees us," Silver said. "We got to get out of town, Steve."

"We got to do somethin'," Harker said. "I just haven't decided what."

# SIX

Clint never did find anything in the house to divert himself with, so he ended up falling asleep on the sofa in the living room. He awoke when he heard the front door open.

"I'm sorry," she said, "did I wake you?"

"No, it's all right," he said. "I was just dozing."

"Where's Billy?"

"Still asleep in one of your guest bedrooms," Clint said. "Poor kid was exhausted. What time is it?"

"Seven," she said. "I closed early because I have houseguests."

"You shouldn't let us interfere with your business."

"That's okay," she said, "It was a slow day, anyway. I just have to wash up, and then I'll make some dinner."

"Hey," Clint said, "you cooked all day. You don't have to do that. We can just—"

"My place is closed," she said, "and that's the best place to eat in town—except for right here. Come on, don't tell me you're not hungry—and when that little boy wakes up he's gonna be starving."

"Well," Clint said, "you're right on both counts."

"I'll check on him and wash up," she said. "It won't take me long. I just need to get the smell of fried food out of my hair."

She left the room and Clint sat back down on the sofa. He didn't hear any voices, so Billy must have still been asleep. It had been hours, now, but that little boy must have been knocked out by his ordeal. It was a wonder he wasn't having bad dreams.

He must have dozed off again himself because the next thing he knew she was coming back into the room. She had removed her dress and put on a robe, and her hair was wet, making it look longer and blacker than before.

"I'll have something cooked in no time," she said. "Why don't you come into the kitchen and keep me company? I'll put some coffee on, first."

"Sounds good."

He got up and walked into the kitchen after her. He noticed the way her body moved beneath the robe and was sure that she was naked under it. She was all woman, with full bosom, hips, and bottom—and she smelled great, not at all like fried food.

He sat at the kitchen table, and she made coffee while telling him a couple of funny things that had happened that day. It was an odd picture. They were almost like a married couple exchanging stories about how their days had gone—only his had a couple of bodies in it.

"Oh, listen to me," she said, putting a cup of coffee in front of him. "I'm babbling on and you and that poor little boy had a horrible day. I'm so sorry."

"It's all right, Sandy."

"I talk a lot like this when I'm nervous."

"What have you got to be nervous about."

"Well," she said, with her back to him, "it's been a long time since I had a man in my kitchen." She looked over her shoulder at him, and he noticed how lovely her eyes were. "I guess that's what's making me a little nervous."

"I could go back into the living room," he said. "Or better yet, I could go to the hotel while you keep Billy here—"

"Oh, that's nonsense," she said, turning to face him. "You'll do no such thing. Besides, that boy worships you. If he wakes up and you're not here, he'll panic."

"He doesn't worship me—"

"How can you not see it?" she said. "It's in his eyes every time he looks at you."

"He's lost his father and mother, Sandy," Clint said.

"And he's latched on to you," she said. She'd started peeling some vegetables while she talked. "I think you're the only thing keeping him from crumbling."

"I've been wondering when he's going to break down," he said. "Or maybe he did his crying already, before I found him."

"How did his eyes look?"

"Bone dry," he said. "No, he hasn't cried yet."

"And he didn't cry in bed," she said. "I checked on him. He must had gone to sleep as soon as his head hit the pillow. He's such a precious little thing."

She finished peeling the vegetables and put them in a pot of water, then took out three steaks she had brought with her from her café.

"Are we eating your stock?" he asked.

"I'd rather give it to you and Billy than to some of the characters who come into my place."

He watched as she prepared the meat to go into a large, iron skillet.

"Clint?"

"Yes?"

"Are you taking Billy to Denver tomorrow?"

"That's the plan."

"And once you get there?"

"I'll find a place for him to stay," Clint said. "A place where they'll take care of him."

"Do you think he'll go without a fight?" she asked.

"Why wouldn't he? He's got nowhere else to go."

"He's got you."

Clint shook his head and said, "I think your exaggerating the way the boy feels about me, Sandy."

"Well, I hope you're right," she said, "for his sake."

# SEVEN

They decided not to wake Billy when the food was ready.

"He just might sleep through the night," Sandy said, "and if he does, it will probably be good for him."

After Clint finished what was possibly the best steak dinner he'd ever had he said, "I have to meet the sheriff over at the saloon."

"To talk about Billy's parents?" she asked.

"Yes." It wasn't entirely true, but the scene between them had become a little too domestic for comfort. At his age this was the closest Clint ever wanted to get to a house, a wife, and children.

"When will you be back?" she asked, and then before he could answer she said hurriedly, "Listen to me, I sound like a wife. The door will be open whenever you come back, and you know where the extra bed is."

"I just want to make sure his parents get a decent burial," Clint said.

"See?" she said. "That's what I meant earlier about you being a special man."

"I don't know about that, but if Billy wakes up and he's, you know, looking for me, will you tell him . . . uh . . . tell him . . ."

"I'll tell him that you haven't gone away," she said. "Don't worry. I'll take care of him."

"I know you will," Clint said. "I'll try not to wake you when I get back."

Clint left the house and walked toward the center of town to find the saloon. He wasn't sure it was the right thing to do accepting Sandy's invitation to stay in her house. It was right for Billy, but not for him. He was beyond the point in his life where he had any hopes for a wife and kids and a home. He was set in his ways and liked the way he lived. Spending time with a woman in a hotel room for one night was one thing, but staying in a woman's home might give her the wrong kind of ideas.

Especially since she thought he was some kind of "special" man.

As Clint left the house Willy Silver remained where he was across the street until he was sure Clint Adams was far away and then Willy crossed to the house. He just wanted to take a quick look around before reporting back to Steve Harker.

When Clint entered the saloon he was instantly more comfortable than he had been in Sandy's house. He looked around and saw that the sheriff was not there yet, so he approached the bar and bought himself a beer.

The place was busy, and from what he'd been able to see it was the only saloon in town. There were a couple of poker games going on at two of the tables, and about three girls were working the floor. There were a few spots open at the bar, but for the most part the place was pretty much packed.

"Passin' through?"

Clint turned and saw the bartender still standing there. Apparently, he hadn't walked away after serving Clint his beer.

"That's right. Why?"

The man shrugged. He was tall and slender and, if you had to guess at his occupation, the first thing that came to mind would have been undertaker.

"Just makin' conversation, friend," the man said. "I see a strange face, that's what I do."

"Well, thanks for the beer," Clint said, "but I'm really not looking for any conversation at the moment."

"Fine with me," the bartender said, his tone insulted, and he turned and walked away.

At that point the bat-wing doors swung in and the sheriff entered. He spotted Clint and came over.

"Couldn't wait, I see," Tyler said.

"A man gets thirsty."

"Gettin' acquainted?"

"I just finished insulting your bartender," Clint said. "Guess I better watch real careful the next time he gets me a beer."

Tyler waved the bartender down and ordered a beer.

"And Hiram?"

"Yeah."

"Mr. Adams is a guest in town," the sheriff said. "His next one's on me, and don't you be spittin' in it."

"Sure thing, Sheriff."

The man didn't sound convincing, though, so Clint figured he'd keep a sharp eye out, anyway.

"Got the boy's parents tucked away safe and sound," Tyler said after a sip of beer. Then he immediately became apologetic. "Sorry, that sounded bad."

"No, it's okay," Clint said. "You didn't know them. Neither did I, for that matter. It's just a shame about the boy, that's all."

"I know," Tyler said. "Is he with Sandy?"

"Yep."

"She might get attached to him, ya know."

"Why's that?"

"Had a boy of her own, for a while."

"What happened to him?"

"Her husband left town and took the boy with him. She's never found out where they are."

"How long ago was that?"

" 'bout four years," Tyler said. "The boy was the same age this boy is now, give or take."

"That's rough," Clint said, "a mother not knowing where her son is. Some women would fall apart and never recover from something like that."

"Yeah, she's a remarkable woman."

Clint thought there was a little more than admiration in the sheriff's tone.

"Still intend to leave early in the mornin'?" the lawman asked.

"Seems advisable, don't you think?"

"I guess," Tyler said. "I find out anything about the

killings, I'll send you a telegram in Denver."

"I'd be obliged," Clint said.

"Sure," the sheriff said, "just like to do whatever I can to help the kid."

# EIGHT

Clint had another beer with the sheriff—watching the bartender closely while he fetched it—and then the lawman went out to do his rounds.

"I'll be in my office early," he told Clint. "Stop by before you leave."

"I'll do that."

Sheriff Tyler left the saloon and Clint turned to the bar to finish his beer.

Earlier in the evening Willy Silver had entered the saloon after taking a good look at Sandy's house. He walked across the crowded room and joined Steve Harker and Dale Madden at their table. Madden pushed a beer across to Silver and said, "Might be warm."

"Long as it's wet," Silver said, picking it up.

"What about the house?" Harker asked, keeping his eyes on Clint Adams, at the bar. He'd been watching Clint since he'd first entered the saloon.

"Nobody there but the waitress and the kid," Silver

said, after a sip of beer. "Be easy to go in and take care of the kid."

"Have to take care of the waitress, too," Dale Madden said. "Couldn't leave her alive."

"You're both wrong," Harker said. "There's who we have to take care of first."

They both looked at the bar.

"Adams?" Madden said. "Why even bother with him, Steve? I'm not lookin' forward to facin' him."

"Me, neither," Silver said. "Why not just take care of the kid and the woman and get out of here."

"If we kill the kid," Harker said, "Adams will never get off our trail. He'll never let up. You're gonna have to face him anyway, so it might as well be on our terms."

"Whataya mean, 'our terms'?" Madden asked.

"He means when and where we say," Silver said, impatiently. He hated having to explain everything to Madden, who was about as dumb as a tree stump.

"Oh."

"And when's that gonna be, Steve?"

"I'm still thinkin'," Harker said.

"About what?" Madden asked.

"About when it's gonna be, stupid!" Silver hissed.

"I was just askin'," Madden said in a hurt tone.

"Why don't the both of you just shut up and let me think," Harker said.

They had a few options, as Harker saw it. They could try to take care of the Gunsmith between the saloon and the house. They could wait until he was in the house and then take care of all three. Or they could let Clint Adams leave town in the morning with the kid, follow them, and take care of them on the trail.

He discarded options one and two. Both would involve the sheriff, and they didn't need somebody else looking for them. Especially if they killed the woman, who lived in town. The people would be in an uproar over that.

No, their best bet was to wait until morning and follow Adams and the boy when they left town and headed for Denver. They had plenty of time and lots of places along the way where they could hit them.

The important thing was that neither of them ever reached Denver alive.

# NINE

Clint let himself into the house as quietly as he could. Sandy had left a light burning for him in the living room, so he wasn't stumbling around in the dark interior of an unfamiliar house. The house was completely on one level, so he extinguished the light and made his way down the hall to the guest room he would sleep in.

He entered and closed the door behind him. He removed his boots, his shirt, and his pants, and then padded around the room in his underwear, looking for a lamp and/or the bed. He found the bed first, figured that would lead him to a lamp, and sat on it. Immediately he realized someone was in the bed and he jumped up, thinking he had entered the wrong room by mistake.

Sandy sat up and turned up the lamp by the bed and stared at him.

"I'm sorry," he said, looking around, "I guess I, uh, came into the wrong room by mistake. I didn't mean—"

"It's all right, Clint," Sandy said. "This is the right room. I—I wanted to talk to you when you got back. I thought it would be easier to wait here for you."

"Oh," he said, relieved. "I didn't want you to think—"

Suddenly, he became aware that he was wearing only his underwear, and he didn't know what she was wearing under the sheet.

"Sandy—"

"Clint . . . it's all right . . . I . . ."

She seemed unsure about what to say next, so she didn't say anything. She got to her knees on the bed and released the sheet. She was wearing a cotton nightgown that tied at the neck. She tugged on one end of the tie and it came undone. The neck of the garment fell away to reveal some creamy flesh, but it was only when she reached up and pulled it down farther that one round, full, pink-tipped breast came free. She slid her hand beneath it, then, cupping it and offering it to him. It was extremely erotic, and he felt his body reacting immediately.

"I know I'm not so young anymore," she said, "but I don't think I'm too bad to look at, do you?"

His mouth was dry, so he wet it before saying, "I don't know, is the other one as pretty as this one?"

She smiled then, a wry, sexy smile that said she knew she had him where she wanted him.

"I don't know," she said, freeing the other breast from the confines of the nightgown. "Why don't you be the judge?"

He came closer to the bed now and reached out for her. She removed her hands so he could cup her breasts, hefting their weight, which was significant and not unpleasant in the least. Her black hair was in a wild tangle around her head, her full lips wet, and at that moment she was probably the most exciting woman he'd seen in a long time. He could smell how ready she was, and that made the whole experience even more heady.

"The boy . . ." he said.

"He's still asleep," she said. "It's as I suspected, he was so tired he'll sleep all night."

"So then we have . . . all night. . . ." he said.

"Oh, God," she said, "that's what I was hoping you'd say. . . ."

He got to his knees next to the bed and lifted her breasts to his mouth. The skin was as smooth as marble, but hot, as if she were feverish. Her nipples were puckered and swollen even before he took them into his mouth. He didn't bother licking them but went right to sucking and then biting them until she moaned and wrapped her fingers in his hair, holding him tightly to her.

He stood then and laid her down, easing the gown completely off of her so he could see her naked body in all its glory. The hair between her legs was as black as it was on her head, and there was a lot of it. He found the sight of that glorious bush intensely erotic. He stepped back and removed his underwear so that his erection pounced free. Her eyes widened and she wet her lips as he joined her on the bed. He laid next to her and kissed her, at the same time running one hand down her body over a soft, sexy belly and down into that tangle of hair until he found her moist and wet. He slid his finger up and down, teasing her as she moaned into his mouth.

"Oooh, God," she said, arching her back, "stop teasing me. I need you now, I need you in me. I have since the minute you walked into the café. God, I was never so . . . so wet just at the sight of a man. . . ."

"Shh," he said.

"Am I shocking you?" she asked. "Do you think I'm . . . nasty? Or dirty?"

"Dirty, no," he said, against her mouth, "but you are nasty, and wicked . . . and you talk too much."

He lifted a leg over her and straddled her. He kissed her again, her mouth, her neck, the slopes of her breasts and then her nipples again, and then he moved his hips so that the head of his penis was right *there,* right at the gate of heaven, and then he poked into her cleanly and hard. She was so wet he slid right in to the hilt. She lifted her legs and wrapped them around him in a powerful embrace, and they began to rock together that way, both biting their lips to keep from crying out because the boy was right down the hall.

Trying to do what they were doing quietly made the whole thing so much more intense. . . .

# TEN

Clint bounded out of bed when he heard the boy screaming, pausing only to pull on his trousers. He burst into the boy's room, found the lamp and turned it up. Billy was sitting up in bed, his eyes wide with fright but unseeing, just screaming and screaming. Clint didn't know what to do, but instinctively sat on the bed and gathered the boy into his arms. He started speaking to him in low tones, trying to reassure him that everything was all right. Billy stopped screaming, but he was still talking, saying the same thing over and over again. That's when Clint realized that he hadn't simply been screaming, but had been yelling, "They're dead, they're dead . . ." over and over again, and now he wasn't screaming it, he was just saying the words over and over, with his face buried in Clint's chest.

Clint continued to hold him and rock him and talk to him and eventually the boy simply wound down and, before Clint knew it, he was holding a sleeping child. Gently he laid Billy back down on the bed and covered him. He stood up, waited a few moments to see if the boy would start yelling again, then turned the lamp down, but not all the way. He wanted to leave some light for the boy in case he woke up.

That done he turned to leave the room and stopped short when he saw Sandy standing in the doorway, watching him. She had pulled on the robe and followed him down the hall.

He held his finger to his lips, and they went back down the hall together to the other guest room.

"Were you watching me the whole time?" he asked.

"Yes."

"I could have used some help."

"I don't see why," she said. "From where I was standing you were doing just fine."

"Fine?" he asked. "I didn't know what I was doing. Look at me, I've been through countless gunfights and none of them ever had me shaking this much."

She went to him, took his hands, and pulled him down so that they were sitting together on the bed.

"You were wonderful," she said. "You were as kind and tender as any father could have been."

"I just . . . did what I could . . . I mean, to calm him down . . . the poor kid . . ."

"And now you have to calm down," she said. "I can feel your heart pounding."

"Well," he complained, "he scared the *shit* out of me. I don't see how parents can do this all the time."

She turned her head away, but not before he noticed her eyes misting up.

"Hey," he said, "I'm sorry. I didn't mean . . ."

"You know?" she asked. "About my son?"

"The sheriff told me. Can't you hire a detective to find them?"

"With what?" she asked. "Hiring a detective is expensive. I don't have that kind of money."

He put his arm around her and said, "I have a friend in Denver who is a detective. He'll do it for free."

"I can't ask you, or him, to do that."

"You're not asking," he said. "I'm offering. I owe you for what you're doing for Billy now."

She put her head on his shoulder and said, "I wouldn't know how to thank you, or your friend."

"First let's see if he can do anything," Clint said. "I'll need you to write down everything you can think of about your husband and your son so I can give it to him."

"I'll take care of that in the morning," she said, "before you and Billy leave."

"Why not now?"

She removed her head from his shoulder and said, "I don't want to waste what time we have left tonight on that."

He pulled her to him to kiss her, but she placed her hands on his chest and pushed.

"Wait," she said. She stood up, grabbed his hands, and pulled him to his feet. "Come with me."

He followed her out of the room and down the hallway. She took him into her bedroom and turned the lamp up. Then she turned down the bed and turned to look at him.

"I want you here," she said. "When you're gone I want to remember having been with you in my bed."

Clint removed his pants and tossed them into a corner. She took off her nightgown and again he was impressed with the fullness of her body. She had the perfect body for sex, but he didn't tell her that. You never know what a woman will think is a compliment and what isn't.

Instead he went to her, and they fell onto her bed locked in a hot embrace. She had him in her hands and her tongue in his mouth, and they writhed against each other, rolled to the center of the bed where they coupled intensely. He slid his hands beneath her to cup the cheeks of her ass and pull her to him every time he thrust into her. She groaned with each stroke, hissed "Yes," into his ear and raked his back with her nails, leaving a trail behind that would stay with him for a while and remind him of her. . . .

# ELEVEN

Clint woke first the next morning and slipped from bed without waking Sandy. He knew if she woke up he wouldn't get out of bed for a while, and he wanted to get an early start. He walked down the hall to check on the boy and was surprised to see the bed empty. He wanted to call out, but that would have awakened Sandy. Instead he went into the living room and found Billy standing at one of the front windows, just looking out.

"Hey, partner," Clint said.

Billy turned and looked at him without smiling.

"I slept a long time."

"Yeah, you did."

"I'm hungry."

"We're going to get you something to eat before we hit the trail, Billy," Clint said.

"I'll make you both something to eat," Sandy said.

Clint turned and saw her standing there, pulling the belt tight on her robe.

"You like eggs, Billy?"

"Yes, ma'am."

"And bacon?"

"Yes, *ma'am.*"

"That's what we'll have, then," Sandy said. "You men entertain yourselves until I call you for breakfast."

Sandy went into the kitchen, and Clint walked to the window to stand next to Billy, who went back to staring outside.

"What are you looking at?" he asked, standing just outside of the window frame.

"A man."

"What man?"

Billy shrugged.

"Just a man."

"What's he doing?"

"Looking at us."

"What?"

"He's just standing across the street, looking at the house."

"Billy," Clint said, "come away from the window for a minute."

Billy turned and looked at Clint.

"How long has the man been there?"

"I don't know. As long as I been up, I guess. He was there when I first looked outside."

"Do you know him?"

"No, sir."

"Ever seen him before?"

"I ain't sure."

"Why not?"

"I can't see his face too clear."

"Clear enough to say you don't know him, but not clear enough to say if you've seen him before."

"Yes, sir."

"All right," Clint said. "Take another look and tell me if he's still there."

Billy looked out the window from between the curtains, then turned back to Clint.

"He's gone."

"But he was there a minute ago?"

"Yes, sir."

"All right, Billy," Clint said. "You keep looking out the window, and tell me if you see him again."

"Yes, sir."

Clint went back down the hall to the room he was supposed to have slept in to get dressed. After strapping on his gun, he went back to the living room.

"Is he there, Billy?"

"No, sir."

"All right," Clint said, "I'm going to go out the back door and have a look around, but I'll be right back. Okay?"

"Yes, sir."

"If you see the man again while I'm gone, you tell Sandy, all right?"

"I will."

Clint went into the kitchen and told Sandy what he was going to do and what Billy was doing.

"Shouldn't you get the sheriff?" Sandy asked.

"No time."

"Why would someone be watching my house?"

"I don't know, Sandy," Clint said, "but maybe I can find out."

"Are you sure you should go alone?"

"There's no other choice," Clint said. "There's no one else to go with me."

"But—"

"You just stay here in the house with Billy and wait for me," Clint said. "I'll be back in a few minutes."

"Be careful."

"I will be," Clint said. "I want my share of that bacon and eggs."

# TWELVE

Clint left the house by the back door and moved around the far side of the building until he reached the front. He peered around the side, but couldn't see anyone. There were a couple of buildings across the street, but they both seemed to be deserted homes. There could have been a man inside watching the house, and that was what he had to find out.

There was a stand of trees off to his right. If he went wide around those trees he could come up behind the deserted houses and take a look at them from the back.

While working his way around he started thinking about who would be watching the house. He supposed it was possible that Sandy had a male admirer who might be watching her, but that would be a mighty big coincidence. It was more likely that it had something to do with him. Maybe somebody had recognized him and was trying to get their courage up to face him.

Never once did it occur to him that someone might be watching Billy.

• • •

By the time Clint reached the back of the deserted homes, Willy Silver was already long gone. He had seen the boy looking out the front window of the house, but doubted that he'd been seen. He did, however, see somebody else moving around inside the house and decided that instead of watching the house it might be better to keep an eye on the livery stable. Before Clint Adams could leave town he was going to have to get his horse. With Silver watching the livery there was no way Adams and the boy could get out of town unseen.

Clint checked both of the deserted houses, and all he found were some stepped-on cigarettes in one of them. Whoever had been watching the house hadn't only been watching it that morning, There were too many dead cigarettes for that. There were enough trampled boot prints in the dusty floor for there to have been more than one man, except for the fact that a worn heel on one of the boots made the imprint very distinctive. Clint figured that only one man had been watching the house, at least since yesterday—the day he and Billy arrived.

He left the deserted house and went back across the street to Sandy's. Billy was watching him from the window. Clint waved, but the boy did not wave back.

At the kitchen table, over bacon and eggs, he told Sandy about the cigarettes and asked her if she had a male admirer who was too shy to approach her.

"Not that I know of," she said. "The types I appeal to generally come right up to me and tell me in no uncertain terms. And usually they just turn my stomach."

"Well, maybe you turned somebody away who hasn't given up," Clint suggested.

"Maybe he's watching you," Sandy said. "Did you think of that?"

"Yes, I did. We got here yesterday and near as I can figure he's been watching since then."

"Maybe he only got here yesterday, too."

"Could be," Clint agreed.

"Or maybe he's watching me."

They were both so surprised at Billy's suggestion that they just stared at him.

"Why would he be watchin' you, sweetie?" Sandy asked.

"Maybe," Billy said, very logically, "he's one of the men who killed my Ma and Pa."

"Billy," Clint said, "you told me you didn't recognize the man."

"I know."

"Were you telling me the truth?"

"Yes, sir."

"Then why do you think he's watching you?"

Billy stuffed bacon and eggs into his mouth and shrugged.

"That's just silly," Sandy said, looking at Clint. "Isn't it?"

"Not necessarily," Clint said. "They did kill his parents—"

"Don't talk about it in front of him," Sandy said.

"Why not?" Clint said. "He already knows all about it, right, partner?"

"Yes, sir."

"If they think he can identify them—"

"Why didn't they kill him in the first place?"

"I ran and hid," Billy said, "like I was told."

"Then how would they know about him, Clint?"

"Somebody here in town could have told them."

"Like who?" she asked. "Who knows besides me . . . and the sheriff? You think the sheriff told them?"

"Let's not jump to any conclusions, Sandy," Clint said. "The sheriff sent two men out to pick them up, and they're over at the undertaker's. Any of them could have told someone else, and it could have got around town that Billy was here."

"I suppose you're right," she said. "What are you gonna do?"

"Billy and I are going to saddle up and leave," Clint said, "just like we planned."

"You'll have to be careful riding to Denver," she said.

He smiled at her and said, "That was my plan, anyway."

# THIRTEEN

Before Clint and Billy left Sandy's house she pulled Clint aside, kissed him, and pressed two pieces of paper into his hand. One was the information regarding her missing husband and son. The other held a name and address.

"What's this?" Clint asked, holding out the second piece of paper.

"It's a place in Denver where you can take Billy."

"What kind of place?" he asked.

"Where they'll take good care of him," she said. "It's run by a friend of mine named Hannah Wells. Just tell her I sent you, okay?"

"Okay, Sandy," Clint said. "We'll stop in and see your friend Hannah."

"And be careful!" she said again, but it was a warning Clint didn't need. He was already planning to ride to Denver with great care, watching his backtrail every step of the way, and keeping Billy very close to him, always.

"And if you ever get the chance," she said, "send me a telegram and let me know how he is."

"I will," Clint said. "I promise."

"And I'll send a telegram to Hannah and let her know you're coming."

They went out to the living room where Sandy asked Billy, "Do you think you could stand a good-bye kiss from me?"

He shrugged and said, "I guess."

She hugged him and kissed him and stood at the door waving to both of them as they walked toward town.

Clint took Billy and stopped in at the sheriff's office.

"Gettin' ready to leave?" Tyler asked.

"On our way to the livery stable," Clint said. "Sheriff, I've got a favor to ask."

"Sure, what is it?"

"Keep an eye on Sandy, will you?"

"Why's that?"

"Well, apparently someone—a man—has been watching her house from across the street."

"How do you know that?"

"Well," Clint said, "Billy saw a man this morning, and I checked it out and found a lot of dead cigarettes on the ground."

"I don't like the sound of that," Tyler said. "You can be damned sure I'll keep an eye on her."

"Good, good," Clint said. "Well, thanks for all your help." Clint shook hands with the lawman.

"Good-bye, young man," Tyler said to Billy.

" 'bye, sir."

"You mind everything this fella tells you," the lawman said, "and he'll get you safe and sound to Denver."

"Yes, sir."

Clint and Billy left the sheriff's office and walked directly to the livery.

They saddled Eclipse but didn't mount up just yet. Clint had noticed that the general store was open early, and he detoured to make a stop there for a few supplies, just some things he could carry in a canvas sack. When Billy spotted a glass jar of licorice sticks and his eyes got big, Clint told him to pick out a few, but to only eat one right now.

"We'll put the others in the sack with the rest of the supplies, and you can have them along the way. How's that?"

"That's just fine!" Billy said enthusiastically.

They carried their supplies outside, and Clint tied the sack to his saddle, then lifted Billy up. Lastly, he mounted Eclipse himself and got comfortable behind Billy.

"You all set?" he asked the boy.

"I'm set."

"Then we're going to Denver," Clint said and headed Eclipse out of town.

"They just left," Willy Silver said when Steve Harker opened his hotel door. Behind Harker Silver could see the big-breasted whore in his bed, looking sort of tuckered out. He grinned, but wiped the grin away when Harker gave him a hard look.

"Get ready to pull out," Harker said. "I'll be done here real soon."

"Shouldn't we get right after him?"

"We've got to give him some room, Willy," Harker

said. "Get ahold of Dale and make sure the two of you are ready to go."

"Oh, we'll be ready," Silver said. He took one last look at the dark-haired whore before Harker closed the door in his face.

Inside, Harker turned and walked to the bed. The big, loose-breasted whore smiled up at him, brushing her hair out of her eyes and licking her full lips.

"Now," he said to her, "where were we?"

She lifted her feet into the air, took hold of her ankles, and spread her legs to remind him.

# FOURTEEN

"Why can't I have my own horse?"

The question came as a surprise to Clint since he and Billy had been riding in silence the entire three hours since they had left Littleton. In fact, it came as such a surprise that Clint was not at all sure he'd heard the boy correctly.

"What?"

"Why can't I have my own horse?"

"Well, for one thing," Clint said, "we never even talked about it."

"Then I can have one?"

"And for another thing," Clint said, "you're too little to handle a horse."

The boy thought that over for a moment, then apparently thought he had the answer.

"Then what about a pony?"

"A pony wouldn't be able to keep up with Eclipse, would he?" Clint asked.

Billy patted Eclipse's neck and said, "No horse could keep up with him. He's great."

"Yes, he is," Clint said, "but let me tell you some stories about a big black horse named Duke. . . ."

Billy was suitably impressed after hearing Clint's stories about his beloved gelding Duke, but he hadn't seen Duke and he was riding Eclipse, and he was nothing if not loyal.

"Duke sounds fine," he said, when Clint was finished, "but I still say Eclipse is the best."

"Well then," Clint said, "I'm not about to argue with you about it."

Clint chose that moment to steal a look behind them. Although he couldn't see their pursuers he knew instinctively that they were there. What his instincts could not tell him is whether they were after him or Billy.

"Why do you keep lookin' behind us?" Billy asked.

"It's a good idea to look all around when you're out riding," Clint said. "Just to be safe."

"You think that man is following us, don't you?" Billy asked. "That he's comin' to kill me?"

"Well, even if someone is following us," Clint said, "they're not going to kill you."

"Why not?"

"Because I'm not going to let them."

"Would you kill them if they tried?"

"I would do whatever I had to do to protect you and me," Clint said, giving what he thought was a safe answer.

"And Eclipse?"

"Oh, yes," Clint said, "and Eclipse."

• • •

As it started to get dark it became apparent that nothing was going to happen on the first day. Clint didn't think they'd come for them in the night, but that didn't mean he wouldn't be on his guard against that eventuality.

When they camped, he showed Billy how to care for Eclipse, and then how to collect wood and start a fire.

"What are we going to eat?"

"Beans."

Billy made a face.

"I don't like beans."

"You'll like them the way I make them," Clint said. "I make trail beans."

"What're trail beans?"

"I'll show you," Clint said, "right after I make myself a pot of trail coffee."

"How do you make trail coffee?"

Clint poured some water into a pot, then a couple of handfuls of coffee and put the pot on the fire.

"That's how you make trail coffee."

"Yuk," Billy said. "What am I gonna drink?"

"Water from the canteen."

"What if we run out of water?"

"We'll refill it in the morning," Clint said. "There's a stream near here. Remember we passed it?"

"I remember."

"Well, it's run up through here a ways, and we'll find it in the morning and refill the canteen."

"Can I have some licorice now?" Billy asked.

"Are you going to taste my beans?"

"Yes, sir."

"Then you can have a piece of licorice while we wait for the beans to be ready. Go on, take one."

Billy hurriedly reached into the canvas sack to snag a stick of licorice, then sat back and watched while Clint combined bacon with the beans to make trail beans.

# FIFTEEN

Billy loved the beans and asked for seconds, which Clint happily gave him.

"It's the bacon," he explained. "It gives the beans a whole different flavor."

After they finished eating, Clint could see that the boy could barely keep his eyes open.

"Come on, partner," he said, grabbing his bedroll. He hadn't thought to get one for the boy, so he figured on just giving him his own. "Let's get you tucked in for the night."

Billy was too tired to argue.

"Clint?" he asked, before nodding off.

"Yeah?"

"Are we really partners?"

"Sure we are, Billy," Clint said. "We're going to be partners all the way to Denver."

"Denver . . ." Billy said. Clint had the feeling that the boy had more questions, but before he could ask them he was asleep.

Clint stoked the fire, put on another pot of coffee, and

settled in for the night. He figured to catnap through it, knowing that he slept light enough that way to be alerted by the slightest sound.

A mile back Steve Harker camped with his two partners, Silver and Dale.

"Smell that?" Silver asked.

"What?" Dale replied.

"He put bacon in with the beans," Silver asked.

"I love it that way," the other man said.

Both men stared accusingly at the pieces of beef jerky they were gnawing on.

"Forget it," Harker said. "We're running a cold camp, and that's that."

"But he ain't gonna smell ours if he's smellin' his," Silver argued, but it was to no avail.

"I don't see why we don't just go in and take care of them now." Dale said.

"That's because you're stupid," Harker said. He looked at Silver. "I'll bet you don't know why, either."

Silver just shrugged and took another bite from his jerky.

"It's a good thing I'm runnin' things," Harker said, "that's all I gotta say."

"So why can't we take care of them now?" Dale asked.

"Because now is when Adams will be especially alert," Harker said. "He would hear the slightest sound near his camp tonight."

"So when will we take care of them?" Silver asked. "I'd like to get on with my life. We got some money off those people in that wagon, and I'd like to spend it."

"Me, too."

"You'll get your chance to spend your money," Harker said. "Tomorrow."

"We can spend it tomorrow?" Dale asked.

"No," Harker said, impatiently, "tomorrow is when we'll take care of them."

"How?" Silver asked.

"Listen up good," Harker said, drawing them in closer, "because I'm only gonna say this once . . ."

Clint tossed some more wood onto the fire, then turned and checked on Billy. The boy was sleeping very comfortably in Clint's bedroll, his face relaxed and serene. He thought what a shame it was that Billy had to grow up without his parents. He hoped that this friend of Sandy's would do well by the boy. Clint had no idea what it must be like to grow up with a loving family, but maybe Billy would still have a chance to find that out. Maybe there was a family somewhere in Denver who was looking for a young boy to love.

He decided that even though Sandy's friend Hannah might run a nice home for boys, he was going to try his best to place Billy in a real home before he left Denver. He hoped his friend Talbot Roper would be able to help.

And he also hoped that Roper might be able to locate Sandy's husband and son, wherever they had ended up living. As sad as it was for a child to grow up without a mother, he couldn't imagine how a mother felt losing her child, not knowing where he was or how he was. Clint thought that Sandy's husband must have been a real bastard to take her son away like that without a word. From the way she'd treated Billy he could see that she must have been a wonderful mother. It was a damned shame for a woman with those instincts not to have anywhere to channel them.

# SIXTEEN

When Billy woke the next morning, Clint treated him to bacon without the beans.

"That's the last of the water," he told the boy. "Finish it, and we'll get some more first thing."

"Can I finish my licorice, too?" Billy asked

"Not in the morning," Clint said. "Let's save that for later, okay?"

"Yes, sir."

After they had saddled Eclipse, Clint lifted Billy into the saddle and mounted up behind him.

"Let's go find that water," Clint said.

"Yes, sir!"

They only had to ride a couple of miles before they found the meandering stream.

"See?" Clint said. "I told you we'd find the water."

He dismounted and helped Billy down, then handed the boy the canteen.

"Go fill 'er up."

"I don't know how."

"It's real easy," Clint said. "You never filled a canteen before?"

"Ma was always afraid I'd fall in the water."

Clint frowned. It seemed the boy's mother might have been trying to keep him a little boy forever.

"Well, come on, I'll show you," Clint said, "and you won't fall in—I promise."

"See?" Harker said, pointing.

He and his two partners were on a rise that looked down on the wandering stream.

"I told you all we had to do was follow the water and they'd be there first thing," he said.

"How'd you know that?" Dale asked.

"Everybody needs water, stupid," Silver said.

"Don't call me—"

"Shut up, the both of you," Harker said. "Do you see that gully over there?"

"Yeah," Silver said, and Dale nodded.

"I want one of you there. I want to get him in a cross fire."

Silver looked at Dale and said, "You go over there."

"Why me?"

"Because I—"

"Goddamnit, Willy," Harker said, "get over in that gully before they mount up and ride away—and don't fire until I do. Understand?"

"I understand."

Silver went, muttering to himself all the way.

"What are they doin'?" Dale asked, looking down at the man and the boy crouched by the water.

"It looks like he's teachin' the boy how to fill up a canteen," Harker said.

"Ha!" Dale said. "That boy don't even know how to put water in a canteen and Willy's callin' me stupid?"

"Just get your gun out," Harker said, from between clenched teeth, "and shut the hell up, Dale."

The first shot went through the canteen, driving it out of Billy's hands and into the water. The boy was shocked and he froze, unable to move.

Clint reacted immediately, and, by the time the second shot was fired, he had grabbed Billy and was carrying him to cover. Lead started chewing up the ground behind him as the outlaws tracked his progress badly. He thanked God that those firing the shots were not better with their irons.

The only cover available was a dry wash nearby, which had probably at one time been part of a creek. It was not even deep enough to be called a gully, but it was deep enough to offer them cover if they laid down flat.

Clint pushed Billy into the dry wash first and then dove in on top of him as the shooting continued. He drew his gun and reserved his fire until he had an actual target.

Once they had gained cover the firing stopped and it got quiet. In the aftermath Clint felt a sting in his leg and looked down to see a wet, red patch on his calf.

And then the pain set in.

"Clint?" Billy said, his voice muffled because his face was in the ground.

"Yes, Billy?"

Billy lifted his head and asked, "Am I shot?"

"No, partner, you're not shot."

"Are you shot?"

The pain from the bullet wound shot up his leg and he said, "Oh, yeah."

# SEVENTEEN

Clint lifted his leg and tied his bandana tightly around his wounded calf. Fortunately, it wasn't debilitating.

"Are you gonna die, Clint?" Billy asked.

"No, Billy," Clint said, "I'm not going to die, and neither are you."

"What are we gonna do?" The boy was obviously frightened, but Clint thought the boy was holding up surprisingly well. Of course, that might have had something to do with the fact that he had already watched his father and mother be killed.

"We're going to get out of here," Clint said, "but if we are you're going to have to do exactly as I say. Understand?"

"Y-yes, sir."

"Good boy."

"B-but—"

"But what?"

"I'm sorry."

"Sorry for what?"

"I'm sorry you got shot trying to save me."

"Billy, I got shot because some bad men are taking shots at us," Clint said. "We don't know why, but we're going to find out."

"Are you gonna kill them?"

"Only if I have to."

Suddenly, Billy seemed to remember something, and he got very agitated—to the point where he tried to raise his head.

"Stay down, Billy!"

"But Eclipse!" the boy said. "Is he all right?"

"He's fine," Clint said. "He knows enough to get himself out of danger. Don't worry about him."

Billy relaxed—as much as he was able to.

"So w-what are we gonna do now?"

"I'm going to have to draw their fire," Clint said, "so I can see where they are."

"How will you do that?"

"I'll stick my head up and one of them will fire at me."

"One?" Billy asked. "There's more than one?"

"There are three."

"B-but, how do you know that?"

"I heard the report of three different guns," Clint said. "One rifle and two handguns."

"You can tell the difference?"

"Oh, yes," Clint said. "After all these years of hearing guns, I can tell the difference."

In spite of the fix they were in, Billy seemed impressed with this.

"You're a very brave boy, Billy," Clint said, ruffling his hair. "Have I told you that?"

"Yes, sir . . . but Clint?"

"Yeah?"

"I'm really very scared."

"I know, Billy," Clint said, "Believe me, so am I."

Harker reloaded his rifle while the others did the same to their handguns.

"I think I got 'im," Dale said.

"If you did it was a damn lucky shot," Harker said. "He moved a lot faster than I thought he would."

"Yeah," Dale said, "you see him run carrying that kid? That looked pretty funny."

"Shut up, Dale, and keep your eyes open."

"Sure, Steve."

Harker shook his head. He was going to have to surround himself with some smarter men when this was all over.

# EIGHTEEN

"Billy, listen to me," Clint said. "Are you listening?"

"Yes."

"You have to stay here, no matter what happens, unless you hear me tell you to run. Do you understand?"

"Y-yes."

"Do you think you can do that?"

"I-I d-don't know," the boy said.

"Well, at least you're honest," Clint said. "Look, if you get the urge to run, they'll shoot you. You don't want to get shot, do you?"

"N-no sir!"

"Then don't run unless I tell you," Clint said. "It's as simple as that. Okay?"

"O-okay."

Clint started to rise, and Billy grabbed his arm with surprising strength for such a little boy.

"Please don't get shot . . . again," Billy said.

"I'm going to do my best."

Clint raised his head until there was a shot.

• • •

"That idiot!" Harker said.

"Who? Willy?" Dale asked.

"Now he showed Adams where he is," Harker said. "You better go over by Willy and tell him to move, Dale."

"What? Now?"

"Yes, now."

"But . . . what if Adams shoots me?"

"Then you'll have the satisfaction of knowing that I'll shoot him right after that."

"B-but—"

"Go!"

Dale frowned, almost a pout, but got up and started to move. . . .

Clint had spotted one man when he saw another man on the move toward the first. Probably to warn him. Or maybe this man was being set up as a decoy. Clint shoots him and another man shoots Clint.

"Billy," Clint said, "I want you to crawl until you can't crawl anymore. When you get to the end of this dry wash, just curl up into a ball and wait for me."

"A-all right."

"Do it now."

Billy started to crawl and Clint began to move back the other way. It was harder for him to move without being seen, and he had to do it flat on his back, using his elbows and his butt. Finally, he reached his end of the dry wash. He'd taken a chance that the man he'd spotted had moved by now, but at least there was distance between him and the boy. He still wasn't convinced that they were after the boy. Maybe, he thought, if they killed him they'd leave the boy alone, but that would leave Billy alone on foot again, like he was after his parents were killed. Could the boy take that a second time?

Clint was determined that Billy would not find out.

"Steve wants us to move," Dale said.

"Why?" Silver asked. "I've got a good bead on the creek and the dry wash from here. I can pick him off when he puts his head up again."

"I dunno," Dale said, "he just said we should move."

"You move," Silver said, "I'm stayin' here."

"I'm goin' back with Steve."

"Go ahead," Silver said, "I don't want you here, anyway."

Dale frowned again, then started back . . . only he never got there.

Clint got a look over the lip of the dry wash without revealing too much of his head. He saw the man moving again, probably between two other men. That meant there were at least three, as he'd surmised from the sounds of the shots.

Clint held his breath, then got quickly to his knees, fired once, and threw himself down again. One of the other men fired two quick shots, and they both impacted in the dirt just above his head, but he'd achieved his goal. The man who had been on the move was still on the move, only this time he was tumbling down from the top of the rise, dead. Clint's bullet had flown straight and true and had taken Dale out of the picture.

Two against one, now. Much better odds.

This wasn't going as planned, Harker thought angrily. Once Adams and the boy got to the water hole they were supposed to die right there at the water's edge. Who would have suspected that all three of them would miss their shots?

Now Dale was dead, and Silver was out of earshot—at least, they couldn't exchange words of instruction without Adams hearing them. There was only one thing for Steve Harker to do.

Get out of there.

# NINETEEN

"Steve!" Willy Silver shouted.

No answer.

"Damn it," he muttered, then tried again, louder. "Steve!"

Still no answer. Harker was either keeping quiet, or . . . he'd left? Pulled out after Dale was killed?

"Steve Harker, you sonofabitch! Are you there?"

No answer.

Shit. Now what?

Clint made the same assumption that Willy Silver did. One of the men—Steve Harker, apparently—had pulled out. That made it one to one, and suddenly all in his favor, because the remaining man sounded angry and nervous.

"Seems like your friend left you!" Clint called out.

No answer.

"Go ahead and pull out, too," Clint said. "I won't stop you."

But he would. He needed to take at least one of them alive to find out what this was about.

"Throw down your gun, and we'll talk," he called out. "You tell me about Steve Harker, and you can go."

Still no answer.

Then . . .

"What guarantee do I have?" a man called out.

"My word."

"You think I'd trust your word?" Silver asked. "A man with your reputation for killing?"

How do you like that, Clint thought. A distrusting bushwhacker.

"Well, either you come down, or I'm coming up," Clint called back.

"Come ahead," Silver shouted. "We'll see who gets out of here alive."

"It won't be you, I can promise you that," Clint said. "I'm coming up the hill."

"You do and I'll cut you down!" To Clint the man sounded almost hysterical. He decided to play on that.

"You've got to be kidding," he said. "You couldn't plug me when I was out in the open, sitting still. How are you going to hit me while I'm coming up that hill after you? You're all alone, and you'll be so nervous you'll never be able to hit me."

Then there was silence, which would only serve to unnerve the man even more. Getting out of this was going to be easier than he'd thought only because the three men hadn't known what to do once they had him pinned down. They didn't know how to work together.

"Okay," Clint shouted, "here I come."

He stood up immediately and started running up the

hill, making a zigzag pattern. The other man also stood and, just as Clint had predicted, he fired uselessly, not even coming close.

And then his gun was empty.

Clint stopped where he was, perhaps twenty yards from the man, who looked like he was going to cry.

"Throw it down," Clint said.

Instead, the man ejected his spent shells and started to reload.

"Don't."

The man continued feverishly. He dropped several bullets, but was managing to get some of them into the gun.

"You're not leaving me any choice!" Clint warned.

"You're gonna kill me anyway!"

"No, I'm not."

But the man was beyond believing him. He finished loading his gun and started to bring it to bear on Clint again.

"Damn it!" Clint said, and fired.

After determining that the man was dead, Clint walked over to where Billy lay curled up into a ball. He stared down at the boy, huddled in the dry wash, and felt even more sorry for him than before. He'd been through a lot in the past few days. More than a boy his age should have to go through in a lifetime.

"Billy."

The boy didn't move.

"Billy, it's me."

Slowly the boy uncurled, as if still afraid that someone would see him moving. When he'd straightened himself out he looked up at Clint, shielding his eyes from the sun with one hand.

"I-is it safe?" he asked in a quavering voice.

"Yes," Clint said, reaching down for him, "it's safe."

# TWENTY

Clint found the horses belonging to the two dead men and went through their saddlebags. He also went through their pockets. He came up with a few items he decided to show Billy.

"Have you ever seen these before, Billy?"

Billy looked at what Clint was holding in his hands. There were two rings and a pocket watch.

"That's Pa's watch."

"And the rings?"

"I-I don't know," Billy said, "but that's Pa's watch."

A boy his age might not have noticed his parent's wedding rings, even if they *were* gold, but that's what Clint thought they were. A big silver pocket watch, though, that was something a boy would notice his father having.

"It's yours now," Clint said, handing him the watch.

"Those men killed my ma and pa?"

"That's the way it seems."

"B-but one got away, didn't he?"

"Yes," Clint said, "but he won't get far."

"How come?"

"Because," Clint said, "now we know his name."

Steve Harker.

When Clint rode into Denver with Billy in front of him on his horse, he was also leading two horses behind him, each holding a dead man tied to the saddle. Riding into a small town like that would raise a few eyebrows, but riding into a city like Denver, this sort of thing was not to be tolerated. Right away someone sent for the police, and then Clint had some explaining to do.

Clint and Billy waited in one of Denver's finer police stations while the police sent a telegram to Sheriff Tyler in Littleton. Eventually a lieutenant named Conrad came up to them as they sat on a long wooden bench in the lobby, under the watchful eye of a desk sergeant. Conrad had Clint's gun belt in his hand and gave it back to him.

"Your story's been confirmed," the man said. He was tall, broad-shouldered, wearing a suit that anyone could see was expensive. In his forties, Lieutenant Conrad had apparently figured out a way to make his lawman's salary stretch further, or he was supplementing his salary with a job on the side. That was no surprise. Wyatt Earp dealt faro to supplement some of his lawman's pay in the past, as had Bat Masterson. Clint just didn't like the look of Lieutenant Conrad and wasn't ready to give him the benefit of that doubt.

Clint stood and accepted his gun belt, strapping it on.

"You know, you shouldn't wear that walking the streets of Denver," Conrad said. "This is a city, not just a town."

"I know that," Clint said. "I'll be staying at the Denver House hotel and my gun belt will be in my room." That didn't mean he'd go unarmed, though.

"And what about the boy?" Conrad asked. "You want us to take him off your hands and find a place for him? Plenty of orphanages around this city."

Clint felt Billy's hand grab his pant leg.

"No, that's okay," Clint said. "I've got plans for him."

"Those fellas you brought in had some money on them," Conrad said. "Too much for the likes of them. I figure they probably got it from the boy's parents. It'll take a little paperwork but I can probably get it released to the boy."

At that moment Clint felt that maybe he had misjudged the man.

"That'd be okay, Lieutenant," Clint said.

"When I get it done I'll bring it to you at the Denver House."

"Thank you."

"You take care, young man," Conrad said to Billy.

"Yes, sir."

"You better get that leg looked at," he said to Clint.

"My next stop."

The lieutenant shook Clint's hand and said, "Well, so long."

Clint and Billy walked out of the police station and stopped on the steps outside.

"Where do we go now, Clint?" Billy asked.

"Well, first we're going to a hospital so I can get my leg taken care of," Clint said, "and then we'll go check into a hotel."

"And after that?"

"Why don't we take it one step at a time, partner?"

"Okay."

They walked down the steps, Clint limping on his injured leg, to where they had left Eclipse, and then Clint decided that they needed a cabdriver to take them to the nearest hospital. He flagged down a passing cab, tied Eclipse to the back of the rig, and told the driver where they wanted to go.

"I'll take you," the man said, "but try not to bleed to much in the back of my cab."

"I'll do my best," Clint said.

# TWENTY-ONE

At the hospital a doctor removed the bullet from Clint's calf and advised him to stay off the leg for a while.

"At least a week, maybe two."

"I'll do my best, Doc."

The doctor bandaged it nice and tight, and Clint felt that as long as it was tightly bound he'd be able to maneuver.

Billy had to wait out in the hall while Clint was treated, and he looked up anxiously when Clint came walking out.

"Are you all right?"

"I'm walking, ain't I?" Clint asked. "I'm fine, Billy. Come on. Let's go check into the hotel and get some food. I'm starved."

"Me, too!"

Billy jumped up off his chair happily and hung on to Clint's hand as they left the hospital.

• • •

Billy's eyes got very wide as they walked into the lobby of the Denver House hotel. Apparently he'd never seen a place so big.

They went to the front desk and, as usual, Clint did not recognize the desk clerk.

And, as usual, no matter who the clerk was, he said, "Nice to have you back with us, Mr. Adams," even before Clint registered. It was something Clint could never understand and was always impressed by.

"I'll need a room with two beds," Clint said as he signed in.

"Certainly, sir. Luggage?"

"None," Clint said, "only these saddlebags. I can handle them."

"Very well, sir," the clerk said. "However, you are limping, sir—"

"I'm fine, really."

"—and you are getting blood on the floor."

Clint looked down and saw that the clerk was right. He had trailed blood across the lobby right from the front door, and people were staring at it, horrified.

"Oh, hell, I'm sorry—" he started to say, but the clerk cut him off.

"It will clean up easily, sir," the man said. "My point was, is there anything we can do for you in light of your, er, injury?"

"You can have someone bring some fresh bandages and tape to my room," Clint said.

"And a doctor?"

"No," Clint said, "just the bandages, thanks. I can take care of it."

"Very well, sir," the man said. "As you wish."

Clint turned to leave the desk, then realized that he

was going to leave a bloody trail all the way up the steps and down the hall, which was carpeted.

"On second thought," he said to the clerk, "maybe your doctor better have a look at it."

"Yes, sir," the clerk said. "This way."

"Didn't they tell you in the hospital to stay off of it?" the doctor asked.

Clint and Billy had followed the clerk to the doctor's office, where the man proceeded to rebandage Clint's leg.

"Yes, they did."

"Well, you better listen to them, then," the doctor said. "You try to do any more walking on this today and it's gonna bleed again."

The doctor finished bandaging Clint's leg nice and tight, and then stood up. He was a well-dressed man in his forties with a little pencil-thin mustache, the kind Clint could never appreciate.

"Thanks, Doc," Clint said. "What do I owe you?"

"No charge for guests of the hotel," the doctor said.

"Thanks, again."

"Send for me if you, uh, need me for anything," the doctor said, walking Clint and Billy to the door of his office. "But neither the hospital nor I will be held responsible if you continue to walk on it."

"I understand, Doc," Clint said. "Thanks."

When they finally got to the room, Billy's eyes got wide again. It was a two-room suite and the bedroom part had two beds in it.

"I get a bed to myself?" the boy asked.

"Haven't you ever had your own bed?" Clint asked.

"Not a real bed."

"Well, now you've got one," Clint said, and then thought, *for a day or so.* Once he got into some sort of home he wasn't sure if Billy would have his own bed. He was spoiling the boy, and maybe that wasn't such a good idea in light of the kind of life he had ahead of him.

"Go ahead," Clint said. "Try it out. I know I'm going to try mine out."

Billy walked to the bed, touched it, then crawled on top of it and laid down on his back.

"How does it feel?"

"Really good."

"Are you tired?"

"Yes?"

"Hungry?"

"Uh-huh."

"Which one more?" Clint asked. "Tired or hungry?"

Billy had to think, then said, "Hungry."

"Okay," Clint said. "Let's just rest a little, and then we'll get something to eat."

"But . . ."

"But what?"

"The doctor said you're not supposed to walk on your leg."

"I know what the doctor said," Clint said, "but part of being grown-up, Billy, is being able to do whatever you want, even if it's the wrong thing."

"But . . . you'll bleed again."

"I won't," Clint said. "We'll only walk down to the dining room, and then come right back up here for the night. How's that?"

Billy didn't seem convinced.

"Hey," Clint said, "we have to eat, right?"

That Billy could agree with.

"Right."

# TWENTY-TWO

Before going into the dining room for dinner, Clint and Billy stopped at the front desk.

"Yes, sir?" asked the clerk who had checked them in.

"I would like to send a note to someone."

"A telegram?" the man asked. "Yes, sir, we can do—"

"No, not a telegram," Clint said. "I want a note hand delivered to someone. I will pay one of your bellmen to do it."

The clerk pursed his lips thoughtfully, then said, "I think we can arrange that, sir. Do you have the note written?"

"Not yet," Clint said. "Do you have some paper and a pencil?"

"Certainly, sir," the clerk said, producing both. Clint wrote a short note to his friend Talbot Roper hoping that the detective was in town and not away on some case. If he was in his office when the note arrived he knew that Roper would respond to it.

"There," he said, handing the note to the clerk.

"When would you like this delivered?"

"Now."

"Very well, sir," the clerk said. "I will see to it."

"What's your name?"

"Vincent, sir."

"Vincent, can I pay you something—"

"Oh, no, sir," Vincent said, holding up his hands, "that will not be necessary. I do whatever I can to make our guests comfortable and happy."

Clint was thinking that most times when a desk clerk had told him that it was followed by the offer of a woman. Not this time, though.

"Okay," Clint said, "we'll be in the dining room having dinner."

"Yes, sir."

"Come on, Billy."

Together they walked into the dining room where they were shown to a table. A waiter was immediately at their side and Clint looked across the table at Billy.

"Would you like a streak?"

"Yes, sir."

"With potatoes?"

The boy nodded enthusiastically.

"And vegetables?"

Billy made a face.

"Two steak dinners," Clint told the waiter, "but hold the vegetables on his. I'll have coffee, and he'll have a sarsaparilla.

"Yes, sir," the waiter said, "hold the vegetables."

As the waiter left, Billy asked Clint, "Who did you send a note to?"

"A friend of mine," Clint said. "His name is Talbot Roper, and he's the best private detective in the world."

"In the world?" Billy repeated, eyes wide.

"Yep."

"What's a private detective?"

Briefly, Clint explained to Billy what Talbot Roper did for a living.

"And is he gonna find Sandy's son for her?"

Clint gave Billy a surprised look.

"How do you know about that?"

"I heard the two of you talking about it."

"What else did you hear us talking about?"

Billy lowered his head and said, "Nothing."

Clint wasn't so sure, but he didn't pursue the matter.

"Well, I'm hoping that he'll be able to find Sandy's son," he said. "We'll have to wait and see."

"When will we find out?"

"It will take a while," Clint said. "First we have to find out if he's even in town, and then we have to see if he has time."

"You can make him do it."

"Why do you say that?"

"People are scared of you."

"What makes you say that?" Clint asked, in a totally different tone.

"Well . . . aren't they?"

Clint considered his reply carefully.

"Maybe some people are, Billy," Clint said. "Some foolish people who believe everything they read and hear, but Talbot Roper is my friend. There's no reason for him to be afraid of me. There's also no reason for me to try to make him do anything."

"But what if he won't do it?"

"If he won't," Clint said, "he'll have a good reason why not."

Billy fell quiet while the waiter came with their

drinks, and when he went away, Billy muttered without looking at Clint, "I still think you could make 'im."

They were only halfway through their dinner when Clint looked up and saw Talbot Roper coming through the doorway.

"Here comes my friend the detective," Clint said to Billy.

Billy turned, looked at Roper, and before the detective had reached the table, Billy said to Clint, "You could definitely make him."

# TWENTY-THREE

Clint immediately found out something about his friend that he'd never known before. Talbot Roper was not good with children. It was obvious that he was not comfortable even sitting at the table with Billy, and the young boy didn't help matters by staring.

Briefly, Clint told Roper how he had come to meet Billy, and why they were together in Denver.

"So what is it you want me to do?" Roper asked. "Find a relative?"

"No," Clint said, "what I'd like you to do has nothing to do with Billy—unless you can suggest a good home for him."

Roper shook his head, stole a glance at Billy, and said, "I wouldn't have the first idea."

"Okay, then," Clint said, "on to the next subject."

He told Roper about Sandy and gave him the slip of paper with all the particulars.

"So she married a guy named Frank Herbert and they had a son named Danny, and the father took off with the son?"

"Right."

Roper looked at Clint.

"Does she have any idea where they might have gone?"

"None."

"Where was this Herbert from, originally."

"I think she wrote that down, too."

Roper frowned at the paper, then said, "Oh, okay."

"Is this something you think you could do for me, Tal?" Clint asked.

"I can certainly make some inquiries," Roper said. "See what I can come up with."

"That's all I'm asking."

"Tell him about gettin' shot," Billy said.

"What?" Roper said. He looked at Billy. "Who got shot?"

"Clint."

"You got shot?"

"In the leg," Clint said. "It wasn't bad."

"He bled all over the floor," Billy said. "They had to clean it up."

"Bled all over what floor?" Roper asked. He looked at Clint. "What's going on?"

So Clint told him about the three men who had killed Billy's parents and then tried to kill Clint and Billy.

"And one of them got away?"

"Right."

"What's his name?"

"Tal, you don't need to get—"

"His name's Steve Harker."

Roper wrote the name down on the same piece of paper with the information about Sandy's son and husband.

"Thanks, kid."

"You're welcome."

"I'll see what I can find out about this Harker fella, too," Roper said. "If he's still running around loose, you better watch your back."

"He wants to kill me," Billy said.

Roper looked at the boy.

"Well, I guess our friend Clint won't let that happen, will he?"

"No, sir."

Roper put the piece of paper away in his jacket and declined the offer of food or beverage.

"I'll get started on this," he said, standing up. "I can find you right here?"

"I'll be here for a while," Clint said. "At least as long as it takes to find a place for Billy to live."

"Sorry I can't help you with that," Roper said. "It's just not something I deal with every day."

"No problem," Clint said. "Sandy gave me the name of a woman who takes in boys. I'll give her a try tomorrow."

"You should stay off that leg for a while," Roper said.

"That's what the doctor told him, too," Billy said.

"Well, the doctor's right," Roper said, "but if I know our friend here, he won't listen."

"My leg is fine," Clint said. "I'll stay off it the rest of tonight and it will be fine."

"Well, that's your business," Roper said. "I can't tie you down, I guess."

"Tal, did you have any plans for this week?" Clint asked. "I mean, am I keeping you from leaving town or working on a case—"

"I'm free," Roper said, "don't worry about that. I've

got a couple of little matters I'm looking into this week, but I owe you too much to let that stand in the way of helping you out."

"I can pay you—"

"Let's not get insulting," Roper said.

"Okay."

Roper looked at Billy and said, "I guess I'll have to count on you to take care of our friend, here."

"I will."

"Well . . . see you both later."

As Roper left the dining room Billy leaned forward and said to Clint, "See? I told you you could make him."

# TWENTY-FOUR

Clint woke before Billy the next morning. His leg was stiff and sore. It would not be advisable for him to walk on it. He didn't need to be told that by doctors, or Roper, or a little boy. Still, he needed to get Billy into decent care somewhere, so he decided that it was worth the risk. All they needed to do today was catch a cab and have the driver take them to the home for boys run by Sandy's friend, Hannah. How much walking would be involved in that? To and from the cab, basically.

He got out of bed and hobbled out to the other room so he wouldn't wake the boy, yet. Let the youngster enjoy his real bed. Who knew what he'd be sleeping on tonight?

Clint was surprised at how well he and the boy were getting on. He had often thought that his relationships with children were on a par with those of Talbot Roper. They were fine as long as they were somebody else's, but often—and disconcertingly—they seemed to be smarter than adults.

Billy was all of that, and yet Clint couldn't help but

feel affection for the little man who had shown so much courage over a short period of time.

"Does it hurt?"

Clint looked up from his chair and saw Billy standing in the doorway. At that moment he had been tentatively touching his injured leg, trying to decide how it would hold up.

"Not too much," he said. "Mostly it's just sore, and a little stiff."

That was another thing about Billy. He seemed to know when Clint was telling him the truth.

"What's it feel like to get shot?"

"It's not a pleasant experience."

"Have you been shot before?"

"Several times."

Billy made a face.

"I hope I never get shot."

"I hope you won't, too," Clint said, "but enough talk about getting shot. How about some steak and eggs for breakfast?"

"That sounds great!"

"And then . . . a bath."

"A bath?"

He ignored the horrified look Billy gave him and got to his feet. Time for them both to get dressed.

After breakfast and Billy's bath, they presented themselves at the front door for the doorman to fetch them a cab.

"Somebody smells real nice," the doorman said, looking down at Billy, who made a face.

"Come on, cheer up," Clint said. "There's no harm in

being clean and smelling nice. I just wish we could have gotten you some new clothes."

"My clothes are fine," Billy huffed.

"Of course they are," Clint said, "you've just been wearing them a while, is all."

When they got in the cab Clint gave the driver the address, and they sat back to enjoy the ride.

Clint had no idea what neighborhood Hannah's house was going to be in, and he wasn't so keen on leaving Billy there when the driver took them down near the docks to a rundown building across the street from a rowdy saloon.

"This is the place," the driver said.

Clint got out of the cab, glad that he had his Colt New Line tucked into his belt at the small of his back, out of sight. The driver left and they turned and walked to the front door of the building. The door had a brass knocker on it and Clint used it. He waited a few moments and then the door was opened by a young woman—a girl, really, probably no more than seventeen. She was thin, but pretty, with long brown hair and great big brown eyes. Clint decided that when she filled out she'd be a beautiful woman.

But this couldn't be Hannah.

"I'm looking for Hannah," Clint said.

"Oh," the girl said, "come in. I'll tell her you're here." She looked down at Billy and smiled, and he saw that he was wrong. She was already beautiful. "How are you?"

"Fine," Billy said, staring at her. Clint believed that Billy was experiencing his first crush.

"Come on in," shc said, and backed away to let them enter, then closed the door behind them.

"I'll tell Hannah you're here," she said, again. "What's your name?"

"I'm Clint Adams," Clint said, "and this is Billy. Hannah's friend Sandy Herbert sent us."

"Oh, yes, Sandy," the girl said. "I'm Angel. Please wait here."

She left them in the entry foyer, which was sparsely and cheaply furnished. He could see a living room, or sitting room, from where they stood, and it also seemed modestly furnished. Clint didn't know where Hannah got her money to run such a place, but if she wasn't spending it on furniture than maybe she was spending it on the boys.

"She's pretty," Billy said.

"Yes, she is," Clint said.

"And Angel's a pretty name."

Clint looked down at the boy, whose face was almost glowing. Yep, he thought, first crush.

# TWENTY-FIVE

"This is the biggest house I've ever seen," Billy said.

"It's big," Clint said. Not huge, as he had been in some very large mansions in the South and in cities like Boston and New York, but to a boy Billy's age, from his background—not that he knew all that much about his background—it would seem huge. It was also not in great condition, from what he had seen of the outside, but at least the inside was clean. He suspected that Sandy's friend Hannah was underfunded.

Angel reappeared and said, "Would you follow me, please? Hannah is in her office."

"Okay!" Billy said, and took off after her before Clint could say a word.

They followed her down a long hall to an open door, and then she stepped aside to allow them to enter.

"Mr. Adams?"

"That's right."

The woman behind the desk smiled and said, "I'm Hannah Wells. Please, come in."

He didn't know what he'd expected Hannah to look

like, but what he got was a competent looking, rather plain woman in her early to mid-forties, dressed very severely, with her hair up in a tight bun and no makeup whatsoever on her face. She extended her hand, which he took, and found himself trapped in a rather firm grip for a woman.

"And who is this?" she asked, looking down at Billy.

"Billy, ma'am."

"Billy what?"

Here it came. Up to now, Billy had not been very forthcoming with his last name, and Clint wasn't sure why. Sure, he'd been real closemouthed in the beginning, but he'd loosened up some since then. His last name was about the only thing he hadn't yet given up.

And he still wasn't.

"Well," Hannah said, "that's all right. We'll settle for Billy, for now. Won't you both have a seat?"

There were two mismatched chairs in front of her desk, one cushioned and one not. Billy sat in the uncushioned one with no fuss. Hannah seated herself behind a desk that was too small for her and folded her hands on top of it.

"Sandy sent you to me?"

"That's right," Clint said. "Didn't she send a telegram to that effect?"

Hannah smiled and said, "Yes, she did. I was just . . . checking. You see, I have very limited space here, and I'm afraid that on occasion I've been forced to turn boys away."

"That's a shame," Clint said. "Where do they go if they can't come here?"

"I'm afraid I can't say."

"Well, how do you manage to pay for this, Miss Wells."

"It's Mrs. Wells," she said, "but you can call me Hannah. As far as our funding, I'm afraid that's a private matter."

Which either meant she didn't want to say, or they were privately funded—or maybe both.

"All right," Clint said. "Did Sandy inform you about what happened to Billy's parents?"

"Yes, she did," Hannah said, "and I can tell you, Mr. Adams, that I'm willing to take Billy on here."

"You can call me Clint," he said, "and if it's a matter of money—"

"It's not," she said. "I'm taking him as a favor to Sandy. Billy?"

"Yes, ma'am?"

"Would you like to stay here with us?"

Billy looked at Clint, and then back at the woman.

"I wanna stay with Clint."

Clint started to speak but Hannah quieted him with a look.

"Well, if you can't stay with Clint, would you like to stay here with us?"

Billy bit his lip and looked at Clint again.

"If you do I can have Angel take you right now and show you where you'll be sleeping."

"Angel?" His eyes lit up. Clint had a feeling he was about to be traded in.

"That's right. Shall I do that? Maybe you can look around with Angel and then decide?"

"Okay!"

"Good. Angel?"

Clint was surprised to find Angel standing at the door.

He'd been under the impression that she had left.

"Come on, Billy," Angel said, extending her hand. "I'll show you around."

Billy jumped down from his chair, took her hand eagerly, then stopped short and looked at Clint.

"You won't leave?"

"Not until you come back down."

"Clint and I will wait here, Billy," Hannah said.

That seemed to satisfy Billy, and he left the room with Angel.

"All of the little boys fall in love with Angel," Hannah said.

"I can imagine."

"Mr. Adams . . . Clint . . . I'll only take Billy on if he decides to stay. The decision has to be his."

"I understand," Clint said. "Hopefully, he'll decide to stay."

"I assume you are not in a position to keep him?"

"Not in a position," he said, "and not of a mind to. I'm no example for a little boy, Mrs.—Hannah."

"Well then," she said, with a professional smile, "let's hope he decides he wants to stay."

# TWENTY-SIX

Clint was sort of hoping that Hannah would ask him if he wanted to be shown around, but she never did. They sat there making small talk, and then suddenly she got a very serious look on her face and asked if she could ask a question. He thought he knew what was coming. Sooner or later the subject always came up.

"You want to know about my reputation," he said. "About whether or not it is well earned."

"Well, I—"

"And you're wondering what a man with my reputation is doing trying to help a small boy."

She scratched her head and looked sheepish.

"I think you caught me," she said. "I was wondering all of that."

"As far as my reputation is concerned, that's other people's doing, not mine," he said. "Word of mouth gets passed, articles appear in newspapers, dime novels appear out of the East and suddenly a man has a reputation that's exaggerated ten times over."

"So you're saying that all I've heard about you is only one tenth true?"

"If that."

"Interesting," she said. "Is that a formula that holds true for everyone? I mean, men like Hickok and Earp and Masterson? Are their reputations also only one tenth true?"

"I'm afraid only they could tell you that, Hannah," Clint said. "I can't speak for them, only for myself."

"I see." She sat back in her chair and took a deep breath. "I fear I've offended you."

"Not at all," he said. "As for Billy, he simply needs help. I found him wandering around the countryside alone, on foot, and I couldn't leave him there. I don't think any man could have."

"I hope that's true," she said, "although I've seen a lot of cruelty perpetrated on children, let me tell you."

"I thought you only had boys here?" Clint said.

"I do," she said. "The only women here are me and Angel. But I have worked with girls in the past."

"So why do you now run a home just for boys?"

She spread her hands and said, "I didn't plan it. It just sort of . . . happened. I simply kept running across boys who needed help, and I finally gave in and made this Hannah's Home for Boys."

"Is that what it's called?"

"That's what I call it."

"This isn't exactly a great neighborhood for the place to be in, is it?" he asked.

"It's what I was able to afford," she said. "You should have seen the place I had before this. At least here I have room to care for twenty or thirty boys."

"That's a lot of boys," he said. "Are they all the same age?"

"Between eight and twelve, mostly," she said. "Again, that's just something that's happened. You'd be surprised how well an eight-year-old can take care of himself on the streets—for a while, anyway."

"I was an eight-year-old once," Clint said, "without parents. I don't think I'd be that surprised."

"Perhaps not," she said. "Ah, I think I hear Billy and Angel coming down the hall."

Clint marveled at her excellent hearing as Billy came rushing in, followed by Angel.

"Clint!" he said, excitedly. "There's lots of boys here my age, and they don't have a ma and a pa, either."

"Is that right?"

"Some of them don't even have ma's and pa's who are dead," the boy went on, "they just . . . didn't want 'em."

"That's a shame," Clint said, not really knowing what to say to the boy.

"Well, how about it, Billy?" Hannah asked.

The boy turned to face her.

"Would you like to stay here with us . . . at least for a while?" she asked.

"Yes, ma'am," Billy said, "but could Clint come visit me?"

"Of course he could," Hannah said. "As often as he likes."

"Will you?" Billy asked. "Come and see me?"

"Sure, Billy," Clint said. "I'll be in Denver for a little while longer, but once I leave . . . I'll come and see you every once in a while."

"You're gonna leave Denver?"

"I don't live here," Clint said.

"Where do you live?"

"I don't really live anywhere, Billy," Clint said. "I just . . . move around."

Then, as if he'd just been struck by a brilliant idea, Billy said, "You could live here!"

"Billy—"

The boy turned and looked at Hannah.

"Couldn't he live here?"

"I'm afraid not, Billy," Hannah said.

"I'm a little too old to be living in a home for boys, Billy," Clint said, "but I'll come and see you."

"You promise?"

"I promise," Clint said, fervently hoping it would be a promise he could keep.

# TWENTY-SEVEN

Clint thought that once he had Billy placed somewhere he'd feel nothing but relief, but by the time a cab had taken him back to his hotel he was actually missing the little guy.

When he entered the hotel he was greeted in the lobby by Lieutenant Conrad.

"Mr. Adams," Conrad said, as Clint approached.

"Hello, Lieutenant."

The two men shook hands.

"What brings you here?" Clint asked.

"I told you I'd try to get that money released for the boy," Conrad said, "remember?"

"I do remember," Clint said. "I just didn't expect to see you this early. Do you have it?"

"Right here," the Lieutenant said, touching the breast pocket of his expensive suit. "Can we, uh, go somewhere so I can give it to you without being a, uh, public spectacle?"

"How about a cup of coffee in the dining room, or a beer in the bar?" Clint asked.

"Coffee sounds good," Conrad said. "I'm on duty."

"Fine," Clint said. "Let's go this way."

Clint led the way to the dining room and they were led to a table.

"Coffee," Clint said, "and a slice of peach pie."

"Lieutenant?" the waiter asked.

"I'll have coffee and a piece of rhubarb," Conrad said.

"I see you've been here before," Clint said, noticing that the waiter had recognized the policeman.

"On occasion."

Conrad took a brown envelope from his pocket and slid it across the table to Clint.

"Here's the boy's money."

Clint had the urge to ask if it was all there, but he decided not to. Even if the lieutenant had taken a little for himself, he was sure the man would act insulted.

"Thank you," Clint said, tucking the envelope away, "I'll see that he gets it."

"Where is the little fella?"

"I placed him in a home for boys," Clint said.

"Ah," Conrad said, "I'm, uh, sure that's best for him."

"I don't know how good it will be for him," Clint said, "but it's got to be better than riding all over the country with me,"

"Are you not completely satisfied with where you placed him?"

"It seems nice enough," Clint said, "but the neighborhood could be better."

Briefly, he described to Conrad where the house was.

"I see what you mean," the policeman said. "Still, if it's what Mrs. Wells can afford . . ."

The statement hung in the air between them and Clint left it there. He did not point out that he had not mentioned the name of the woman who ran the house. But Conrad was a policeman, and perhaps he knew the place Clint meant just from the description.

"Well, this money should help," Clint said.

"You'll give it to her?"

"She's taking care of the boy," Clint said. "It seems like the right thing to do."

"I suppose a place like that could always put some extra money to use."

"Definitely."

The waiter arrived with their coffee and pie, and they suspended the conversation until he had served them and left.

"So, does this mean you'll be leaving?" Conrad asked. He seemed to be trying to make the question sound as offhanded as possible, but wasn't succeeding very well.

"Not right away."

"Oh?"

"I have a friend in town I'd like to see."

"Anyone I'd know?"

"Probably," Clint said. He thought about leaving it at that, but relented. "Talbot Roper."

"The private detective?"

"That's right."

"And he's a friend of yours?"

"Yes," Clint said, "a longtime friend."

"So your visit with him would be for . . . pleasure?"

"That's right," Clint said, "just a friendly visit."

"I see," Conrad said. "Well, I understand he's a very busy man. I hope he's in town for you to see."

"I hope so, too."

The two men finished their pie and coffee over small

talk and then walked back out to the lobby, where they parted company over another handshake.

"I appreciate you taking the time to bring the money," Clint said.

"Not at all," Lieutenant Conrad said. "I hope the little fella is happy where he is."

"I'm sure he will be."

Conrad left, then, and left Clint Adams wondering. . . .

# TWENTY-EIGHT

After Conrad had left, Clint went up to his room for a while. Having a child around with you all the time was exhausting. He didn't know how parents could do it. He took off his boots, laid down on the bed, and fell asleep.

Bob Conrad knew he'd made a mistake when he referred to Hannah Wells as "Mrs. Wells." Clint Adams had not mentioned Hannah's name at any time. Of course, knowing her name didn't make him guilty of anything. Also, he hadn't taken any of the money that had been recovered for the boy because he had no way of knowing whether or not Clint knew how much there was to begin with. Besides, there really wasn't that much, and Clint Adams was going to give it to Hannah anyway.

Hannah Wells was known to those who *really* knew her as Coldhearted Hannah. She was especially coldhearted when it came to Lieutenant Bob Conrad, and he didn't know why. But the nickname was given to her by the people who knew what she really did with the boys who lived in her care. She certainly did not take the boys in from the warmth of her heart, that was for sure.

Conrad left the Denver House hotel and went directly to what he always thought of as Coldhearted Hannah's Home for Wayward Boys.

"Where's the boy?" Conrad asked when they were alone in her office. The delicious Angel had shown him the way, and all the way down the hall he had watched her taut butt undulate underneath her dress. She was going to be something when she got a little older.

"Quiet!" Hannah said, and closed the door so that no one could overhear them. What she didn't know was that Angel had perfected the art of eavesdropping. As soon as the door clicked shut she was there with a glass pressed to the door and her ear pressed to the glass.

"Well, where is he?"

"He's upstairs, with the others."

"What if they say something to him?"

"They won't."

"Why not?"

"Because they know they'd get in trouble if they did," she told him. "Calm down and tell me why you're so worked up."

"Clint Adams," Conrad said, sitting down. "You do know who Clint Adams is, don't you?"

"Some kind of legend," she said, offhandedly. "What's that got to do with us?"

"If he finds out what we're doing here—"

"Why should he find out?"

"From the boy."

"Look," Hannah said, sitting back in her chair. "Adams is going to be done, soon, leaving the boy in my care. A few days after he leaves, the boy will have an accident."

"And what will you tell Adams?"

"Why do I have to tell him anything?" Hannah asked. "He'll probably never come through here again."

"Think again," Conrad said. "He has friends here."

"Who?"

"Talbot Roper, for one."

Now she sat forward, a frown on her face.

"I don't like the sound of that," she said. "Roper could be troublesome."

"I know. So if Adams does come back to see the kid?"

"He'd probably write him first," she said. "I could send a letter back telling him about the accident."

"Which would probably bring him running here."

"You think he and that boy are that close?"

"You tell me," Conrad said. "You saw them here together."

"The boy fell in love with Angel, like they all do," she said, tapping her front teeth with a fingernail. "He did, however, make Adams promise to visit him."

"See?"

Hannah got up and started to pace.

"You never should have taken the boy in," Conrad said.

"Oh, sure," she said, "that would have looked good. They were sent to me by a friend, and I turn them away."

"And what the hell is wrong with Sandy, anyway? Why'd she send them here?"

"Ah," Hannah said, "her telegram said the boy reminded her of her son."

"Great," Conrad said. "She's got too soft a heart."

"Most women do," Hannah said.

"Not you, though."

"No," she said, turning to face him, "not me. Do you know what has to happen now, Bob?"

"What?"

She walked over to where he was and stared down at him.

"Both Adams *and* the boy are going to have to have an accident," she said, stroking his jaw, "and that's going to be your responsibility."

# TWENTY-NINE

Clint was standing at the bar in the Denver House when Talbot Roper came in. Roper had left a message for Clint at the front desk that he would be coming to the Denver House for dinner. His note also said that the dinner would be "on you."

"I'm ready for a steak," Roper said.

"How about a drink first?"

"I'll have a beer with the steak."

"Okay," Clint said, "I know a hungry man when I see one."

They left the bar and went into the dining room, where they each ordered a beer and a steak dinner.

"I'm not here to tell you that I've found out anything," Roper said.

"I didn't think you were," Clint said. "It's a little too soon, even for you."

"I have feelers out, though," Roper said. "If they're out there to be found, I'll find them."

"I know you will."

Roper sat back in his chair and regarded his friend in

silence for a few moments. Clint instinctively knew the man had something on his mind, so he waited.

"You have a lot faith in me, don't you?"

"You're the best," Clint said simply, as if that explained it.

"I know," Roper said, immodestly. "In fact I'm so good I'm getting too busy."

"That's a complaint?" Clint asked. "Being too busy? What, are you making too much money?"

"That's just it," Roper said. "I'm losing money,"

"How so?"

"I'm having to turn jobs away because I don't have the time to take them."

"Well," Clint said, "the answer to that is simple."

"Enlighten me."

"Take a partner."

Roper smiled.

"Oh, no . . ." Clint said, realizing he'd just been manipulated by a master.

"Oh, yes," Roper said.

"Not me."

"You," Roper said, with a nod.

"I'm not a detective, Tal."

"You have the best instincts for it of anyone I've ever met," Roper said. "You could be better than me."

"Not better then you."

"All right," Roper relented, "maybe not better than me, but as good as."

"I doubt that—"

"I thought you had faith in me."

"I do, but—"

"Then you have to have faith in my opinion," Roper

said. "It's my opinion that you'd make a great private detective and a great partner for me."

"You'd never convince Alan Pinkerton of that first part."

"Pinkerton had no idea what he had in me, and he won't see the potential in you. I do."

"Tal—"

Roper held his hands up and said, "Why don't you think it over for a while? At least, for the rest of the time that you're here."

"Tal—"

"We could make a lot of money together, Clint," Roper said, "and do a lot of good."

"You're trying to manipulate me . . . again!"

"Okay," Roper said, "manipulation is over." He pointed his index finger at Clint and leaned forward. "But you know I'm right. We've worked together well in the past."

"Yes, we have, but—"

"There you are," Roper said, sitting back again. "I'm through selling now. I'll just let you think about it for a while."

At that point, the waiter appeared with their dinners and they both started eating, which took most of their attention because the steaks at the Denver House were huge.

After dinner they had pie and coffee and talked about things other than a possible partnership.

"I had a visitor today," Clint said.

"Who?"

"Somebody who knows who you are."

"A policeman?"

"Right."

"Which one?"

"Conrad, a lieutenant."

Roper put his fork down.

"He's a bad one, Clint."

"Well, his clothes are too good for him to be completely honest, but—"

"No," Roper said, "I mean, he's really a bad one."

Clint studied his friend for a few moments and saw that he was dead serious.

"Okay," he said. "Tell me."

# THIRTY

"Well, for one thing," Roper said, "he's a killer."

"That's been said about me," Clint said. "If he is, why is he on the police force?"

"Because no one can prove it," Roper said, "but my sources are good. There have been times when he has simply executed someone."

"Why?"

"Because he can't prove they're guilty," Roper said, "but he knows they are."

"Sort of the way you feel about him."

Roper smiled.

"Ironic, isn't it?" the detective said. "This is all beyond the fact that he's as crooked as they come. He's got friends in power, Clint, and they've given him a badge, which to him is the same as a license to steal."

"You don't like him."

"Not one bit."

"I sensed he feels the same way about you."

"He knows I'd put him away if I could."

"But he's too smart?"

Roper hesitated, then said, "Let's say he's been too smart up to now and leave it at that."

Sensing that his friend's pride might have been stung once or twice by the lieutenant, Clint said, "Okay. . . ."

They finished their meal and adjourned to the bar for more drinks. Roper lit a cigar without offering Clint one, knowing his friend was not a cigar smoker. Clint would, however, occasionally accept one when it was offered. Roper's, however, were too good to waste on an occasional smoker like Clint, so he took no offense.

Roper got his cigar going, and they remained at the bar when the bartender brought their beers. The bar at the Denver House was a quiet, peaceful place to drink. There was no gambling and no girls, only beer and whiskey and some quiet conversation.

"You get that boy placed?" Roper asked.

"This afternoon."

"Where?"

"He's with a woman called Hannah who runs a—"

"Hannah Wells?"

"That's right. You know her?"

"I know Hannah," Roper said.

"Well?"

"Well enough to suggest to you that you get that boy out of there as soon as you can."

"Why?"

"Because he'll learn the wrong things from Hannah."

"Like what?"

"Like picking pockets."

"What?"

Roper nodded. "Why do you think she picks only boys?"

"To train them as pickpockets?"

"Pickpockets, petty thieves, whatever you want to call them," Roper said. "That's how she gets her money."

"And if you know this, who else does?"

"You mean the police?"

Clint nodded.

"Oh, they know."

"So why don't they shut her down?"

"She's got protection."

"In the police department?"

Roper nodded.

"Who?"

Roper smiled. "Who do you think?"

# THIRTY-ONE

"Are we finished?" Conrad asked.

"No," Hannah said. She walked to the door and locked it, and he knew what was coming next. He was already getting excited.

She walked to where he was sitting, pulled him to his feet, and backed him up to her desk. She undid his belt and pulled down his trousers and underwear. His penis was already semierect when she got down on her knees and took it into her mouth. She sucked it expertly, greedily, until it was as hard as she could get it, and then she stood up and pushed him onto his back on her desk. She pulled her skirt up and pulled down her own undies, then climbed on top of him and took him inside of her.

She was so wet that he slid right in, and the heat of her engulfed him. She began to ride him up and down and he gritted his teeth as he watched her face. This was the way they had sex, when she wanted it and on her terms. Most of the time he never even saw her naked breasts, but most of the time he didn't care. This was exciting. He never knew when she was going to want it, but when she did she was voracious and insatiable. She rode him up and down, biting her lip to keep from crying out. He watched her face as he always did, enjoying the way her lips became swollen, her face became red, the way she shut her eyes, the way her nostrils flared, and the cords on her neck stood out. . . .

Every so often she took him to her bed and he was able to enjoy her fully, but for the most part their couplings were like this. She didn't love him, he knew that, and he didn't love her. In fact, he knew that for her there was no emotion involved in what they were doing. But every so often she needed the release. He didn't even know if he was the only one she used when she got the urge, but he didn't care. Bob Conrad was obsessed with Hannah Wells and he was happy to be used by her whenever she wanted. He saw the Hannah nobody else saw, the one without the bun, the one who was riding him now, straining for her release, the one who didn't look so prim and proper anymore. He loved the smell that filled the air when they were rutting like this, the comingling of their scents. It was a smell that came to him every so often during the day, and sometimes at night, and whatever he was doing he would stop . . . and then it would be gone. Sometimes he looked around to see if she was there, but she never was. The smell was in his head, in his memory, his subconscious, and every so often it worked its way to the surface and got his attention.

He could feel the muscles in her thighs as she rode him, and then her insides were gripping him, milking him, and suddenly his own release was being yanked from him. He grunted, keeping as quiet as he could be, and she was completely soundless as he felt her begin to spasm . . . and then they were done, and she was off of him, smoothing down her skirt.

He sat up and got off her desk before she could tell him to. He pulled his pants up, trying to catch his breath at the same time. It was over, but he could still feel her wetness on him, and that smell was still in the air.

"Now we're done," she said without any emotion. "I want Adams taken care of."

"I know just the man for the job," Conrad said.

"Then get it done," she said, "and let me know when it is. Let yourself out."

He finished arranging his clothing, then turned, unlocked the door, and left.

Just before Conrad unlocked the door Angel removed her glass turned, and ran down the hall. She hid in a closet as Conrad walked by. She heard the front door open as he left the house. She stayed there a while longer, waiting for her breathing to return to normal. There was a tingling between her legs, but she dared not touch herself there. This always happened when Hannah and the policemen were together. Angel would be outside the room, whether it was Hannah's office or her bedroom, listening. They thought they were quiet, and they were as far as the rest of the house was concerned, but Angel could hear them. She could hear their little grunts and groans, and the sound their bodies made rubbing and bumping against each other.

One day, she thought, she would reach down and touch herself there, and she wondered what would happen when she did?

• • •

When she was alone, Hannah Wells slid her hand beneath her skirt and dipped her fingers into herself, where his juices still flowed from her. She lifted her fingers to her nose and sniffed, smelling them both there. She closed her eyes and breathed the scent in deeply. She wet her lips and put her head back, remembering how he had felt inside of her. Next time, she thought, she would let him have her naked breasts. She would tell him to bite her nipples hard so that they would still be sore days later. So that whenever she moved and her clothing rubbed against her she'd remember how they'd been together. . . .

She could never let Conrad know how much she enjoyed what they did. She could never let any man know that she liked it.

She could barely even admit it to herself without feeling shame.

# THIRTY-TWO

"I should go and get him out of there now," Clint said.

"Tomorrow is time enough," Roper said.

"But if she's what you say she is—"

"She's not going to teach him to pick pockets in one night, Clint," the detective said. "He's safe for now. Just get him out of there as soon as you can."

"I've got to find a place to for him to stay."

Roper sighed and said, "I'll ask around, see if anyone wants a kid—although why they would I'll never know. More trouble than they're worth, if you ask me."

"This one's okay," Clint said.

"So you keep him, then."

"Well," Clint said, "let's not get carried away. He's okay, but he's not that okay. He's still a kid."

"Well," Roper said, "you could leave him with Hannah. I mean, she'd teach him to steal, but she'd probably treat him pretty well. He'd have a bed and three meals a day, and when he got too old he could leave and go out on his own."

"Into business for himself, you mean."

"Well . . . yeah . . ."

"Stealing."

"Hey," Roper said, "if he was good at it he could do pretty well for himself."

Clint frowned at his friend and said, "You sound like you're speaking from experience."

"I did my share of stealing when I was a kid," Roper said. Clint realized then that he didn't know much about Roper's childhood, but prying now would create a tit-for-tat situation, and he wasn't quite ready for that.

"I suppose we all have," he said, and let the matter drop. "But I don't think I'll leave him to live that kind of a life. If he wants to do anything like that he can make up his own mind when he's old enough."

"Okay, then how about this?"

"What?"

"What will you do if he doesn't want to leave?"

"He's only been there one night."

"In a bed," Roper said, "with other boys his own age. And then there's Angel."

"You know about Angel?"

"Hannah Wells's secret weapon," Roper said. "Angel keeps the boys in line because they're all in love with her. They all think they're gonna grow up and live with Angel."

"He's just a little boy, Tal."

"You saw his face when he saw Angel, didn't you? I'll bet his face lit up."

Clint had to admit that it had.

"So he's in love with her already," Roper said. "So you go there to get him tomorrow, and he says he doesn't want to leave. What will you do?"

"I don't know," Clint said. "Force him, I guess."

"Force him?" Roper said. "All that will do is make him want to go back all the more."

"Well, then, I don't know what I'll do," Clint said. "I suppose I'll have to cross that bridge when I come to it, won't I?"

"I guess so," Roper said. "I've got to get going. Thanks for the meal and the drinks. I'll get back to you as soon as I know something solid about Sandy's son."

"Okay, thanks."

"I'll give you one piece of advice before I leave."

"What's that?"

"Think about what you're going to do tomorrow," Roper said. "Consider every eventuality. Don't go up against Hannah Wells without a plan, because if you do, you'll lose."

"I can believe it," Clint said. "She impressed me as being very much in control."

"She is. Just ask Conrad. She leads him around by the nose."

"I would have thought he was in with her for the money," Clint said.

"Think again," Roper said. "The Hannah Wells you saw is not the one he knows. Take my word for it."

"Okay," Clint said. "Thanks for the advice."

Roper nodded, waved, and left the bar and the hotel. Clint turned to face the bar and the bartender fronted him.

"Another one?"

Clint looked down at the warm remains of his beer, then pushed the mug across the bar.

"Why not?"

Clint nursed this last beer before going up to his room. He took it to a table and drank it slowly, thinking about Billy and what he might have dropped him into. If Roper was right—and Clint had no doubt that he was—then it was his responsibility to get the boy out of there, one way or another.

However, Roper had a good point.

What if Billy didn't want to leave?

Billy thought that the bed he had slept in when he was at the hotel with Clint was much more comfortable than this one. But this one was more comfortable than anything he'd ever had before the one in Clint's room. And at least here he had his own bed, and he had friends. He had only been there a short time, but already he had friends named Danny and Sam and Eddie. They were about his age and they told him he was really gonna like it there. They got to do lots of things parents wouldn't let them do. When Billy asked what things, they just told him that he'd see soon enough.

And then there was Angel. She sure did have a pretty face, and she smelled good, too. Billy didn't know he had a crush on her because he'd never had a crush on a girl before. He just knew that he got a funny feeling in his stomach when he saw her, and it wasn't a bad feeling, either. His new friends told him that they all felt like that around Angel.

And the best thing was that Angel had tucked them in, every last one of them. And she had paid special attention to Billy, making sure his blankets were tucked in right and even kissing him on the forehead like his momma used to—only he never felt with his mother the way he did when Angela kissed him.

Billy didn't know what was going on, but he knew he was glad Clint had brought him here.

# THIRTY-THREE

After Lieutenant Conrad left Hannah Wells's, he didn't go far, just across the street and down the block to a small saloon that catered to a certain clientele. They had to know you there for you to get past the front door, and if you happened to get in, and they didn't know you, there was very little chance of you getting out.

They knew Conrad, and he was the only cop that was ever allowed to get past the front door.

"Hey, Lieutenant," the bartender greeted him as he entered.

It was late, but the place was small and it didn't take that many patrons to fill it. It was filled now, and they all knew Conrad, knew he was a cop, but knew he was one of them.

"Beer," Conrad said, "at that back table, the one with the sad lookin' guy sitting at it."

"He's been here a while," the barman said, drawing the beer. "Waitin' for you?"

"Yep."

"You better bring him a cold one, then," the bartender

said, drawing another one. "He's been nursing that one a long time."

"Thanks."

Conrad picked up both beers and walked to the table in question. He put one beer down in front of the man sitting there, then sat across from him with the other beer.

"Don't look so down," he told the man. "You're going to get a chance for some revenge."

"Revenge for what?" the man asked.

"Your friends," Conrad said, "your partners."

"I ain't lookin' for any revenge for them," the man said. "I've still got me to worry about."

"Well," Conrad said, "I'm going to give you a chance to stop worrying and do something to help yourself."

"Namely what?"

"Namely," Conrad said, "kill Clint Adams."

"I ain't facin' the Gunsmith—"

"I didn't say face him," Conrad said, "I said kill him. There's a big difference."

"Yeah?"

"Yeah," Conrad said,

"Tell me more," Steve Harker said, suddenly interested.

# THIRTY-FOUR

When Clint woke in the morning he looked over at the empty second bed and thought about Billy. He had to get the boy away from Hannah Wells today. The only thing he still couldn't understand was why Sandy would send him and the boy to somebody like Hannah. Of course, it was possible that Sandy didn't know what Hannah was teaching the boys and using them for. Yeah, that had to be it.

He got up, washed, and got dressed. The last thing he did before leaving the room was tuck the Colt New Line into his belt at the small of his back, then put on a jacket to cover it.

He left the room and headed for the dining room.

Steve Harker waited patiently across the street from the Denver House hotel. Conrad had told him that shootings had taken place before in front of the hotel. Famous people often stayed there, the detective had told him, and no one would really be surprised when Clint Adams was gunned down on the street.

He thought back to his conversation with Conrad the night before, when the policeman had told him where Clint Adams was staying. . . .

"What about the rest of your people?" Harker asked. "After I kill Clint Adams, are they just gonna look the other way?"

"Don't worry about that," Conrad said. "I'll be handling the investigation."

"And what about the kid?" Harker asked. "Look, I was told that you helped fellas like me out."

"You were told right," Conrad said. "I'm sure you were also told there was a price."

"I got money."

"I don't want money," Conrad said. "I want you to take care of Clint Adams for me."

"And what about the boy?" Harker asked. "Who's gonna take care of the boy so he don't identify me?"

"Don't worry about the boy," Conrad said. "He's in good hands, He's being taken care of."

"I don't want him pointing the finger at me—"

"Nobody's going to put the finger on you, Harker," Conrad said. "I guarantee it."

Harker looked both ways. It was early, and there wasn't that much foot traffic on the street. From his vantage point in the doorway of a shop that had not opened yet, he had a clear view of the front door of the hotel, and therefore a clear shot at Clint Adams when he came out.

Then he saw Lieutenant Bob Conrad walking down the street toward the front door of the hotel.

"What the hell is he doing here?" he asked himself, aloud.

• • •

Clint saw Conrad enter the lobby of the hotel and look around. When he saw Clint he gave a friendly little wave and started toward him. Clint recalled the things Roper had said about Conrad, but as much as he trusted Roper, he had decided to form his own opinions about the man. Clint always gave people an opportunity to make their own impressions on him before he judged them.

But he wasn't doing that with Hannah Wells, was he?

"Mr. Adams," Conrad said as he got closer.

"Just call me Clint." The two men shook hands. "What brings you here this morning, Lieutenant?"

"Just something I wanted to discuss with you," Conrad said. "Can I walk with you and discuss it?"

"Sure, why not?"

They headed for the front door.

"Where are you headed today?"

Clint considered his answer and then thought, why not?

"I'm going to get the boy, Billy, back from the place I left him," Clint said.

"Why is that?"

"I've heard some disturbing things about the woman whose care I left him in."

"And who was that?"

"Hannah Wells."

"Coldhearted Hannah," Conrad said with a nod.

"What?"

"That's what they call her," Conrad said, as they stepped out the front door, "and her place is know as Coldhearted Hannah's Home for Wayward Boys."

That surprised Clint. He'd expected the policeman to

either deny knowing her or rush to her defense.

"I wish I'd known that before I took him there."

"Oh," Conrad said, "I forgot. I had to ask the desk clerk something. I won't be long."

Clint stepped out the door, turned, and watched the lieutenant hurry across the lobby. What did he have to talk to the desk clerk about? Him? Or another guest?

He turned back in time to see a man across the street raise a gun and point it at him, and then his instincts took over.

# THIRTY-FIVE

The first bullet shattered glass, which crashed inward and across the hotel lobby floor like ice. Conrad turned, expecting to see Clint Adams lying amidst the glass, a bloody mess, but there was no sign of him.

There was a second shot, and then Conrad was running for the door. If that fool Harker missed, and Clint Adams caught him . . . Well, he had to make sure that didn't happen.

Clint hit the ground just as the first shot was fired. It struck the glass behind and above him, but there was no danger to him because the glass shattered inward.

He rolled as he hit the ground, reaching behind him and beneath his jacket for the Colt New Line, which would be of no use at this range except as a noisemaker. He was going to have to get closer.

As he started to get to his feet he noticed two things. One, the shooter was now running down the street and, two, Lieutenant Conrad was coming out of the front door of the hotel.

"What happened?" Conrad called out.

"Someone took a shot at me."

"Where is he?"

"Come on," Clint said, "follow me."

He took off down the street after the shooter, with Conrad close on his heels.

He was able to keep the man in sight because he was running erratically, as if he didn't know where he wanted to go. Maybe he didn't. Maybe he wasn't familiar with the streets. That would work in Clint's favor because he did know the streets of Denver.

And so did Conrad.

"I'm gonna cut him off!" the policeman yelled, and changed direction while Clint continued to pursue the fleeing man.

Steve Harker was very confused. It seemed that not only was Clint Adams pursuing him, but Lieutenant Conrad as well! He'd only gotten one clear shot at Clint Adams, but the man seemed to sense that he was there and he had missed. The second shot was hurried, and he didn't have time for a third. Now all he wanted to do was escape.

He turned a corner, not knowing where he was going, and suddenly there was Conrad in front of him, holding a gun and pointing it at him!

"What are you doing?" he managed to cry out before the man shot him.

Clint turned the corner and saw the shooter running right into the arms of Conrad.

"No!" he shouted. He wanted to take the man alive and find out why he had been shooting at him, but he knew it was too late. The man shouted something at the policeman, who then fired. The bullet took the man right off his feet and onto his back. By the time Clint reached him he was dead, eyes staring sightlessly at the sky. Conrad joined him.

"Know 'im?" he asked.

"As a matter of fact, I do," Clint said. "His name's Harker. He was the leader of the man who killed Billy's parents."

"Well," Conrad said, "seems you got the other two, but I got this one for you."

Clint looked at Conrad. It seemed to him they might have taken Harker alive. He had probably spotted Clint on the street, or coming out of the hotel, and panicked, but Clint would still have liked to talk to the man. Conrad, on the other hand, seemed in a hurry to kill him.

"Seems you did," Clint said.

"He must have spotted you and panicked," Conrad said. "Or maybe he saw you yesterday and decided to wait for you to come out today."

"Either way," Clint said, "we won't know for sure, will we?"

Conrad frowned.

"You saying I was a little quick on the trigger?"

"I'm not saying—"

"This man was running down a crowded street with a gun in his hand," Conrad went on. "I wasn't about to take any chances. I did my job as I saw fit."

"What about your question?"

"What?" Conrad looked confused.

"The question you went back into the hotel to ask the desk clerk," Clint said. "Don't you still need an answer?"

Conrad frowned, then took a moment to put his gun away in his shoulder holster.

"You know," he said, putting his hands on his hips, "in all the excitement I pretty much forgot what the question was."

Clint wasn't surprised.

# THIRTY-SIX

Clint left Lieutenant Conrad to take care of the removal of the body. Since he himself had not fired a shot, he was not involved.

"We can talk later," Clint said.

"Later?"

"Whatever it was you wanted to talk to me about."

"Oh, right, that," Conrad said. "Well, it'll have to wait until I clear this mess up."

"Fine," Clint said, and left.

He was convinced that not only had Conrad set him up with Steve Harker, but had made sure he was there to take care of Harker if the man failed, which he certainly did. Clint knew that Harker had been shouting something at Conrad just before the policeman shot him. He was probably shocked at what was happening to him.

Clint returned to the hotel. He decided to send a message to Talbot Roper, once again using a hotel bellman to deliver it. This one was very simple. It read: "Need backup." Clint knew that as soon as Roper received it, he would be on his way.

• • •

Clint decided that it was too dangerous for him to go back to Hannah's alone. According to Roper, Conrad was at Hannah's beck and call. He couldn't take a chance on walking into a trap, so he'd wait for Roper and they'd come up with a plan to get Billy away from Coldhearted Hannah's.

Clint was feeling pretty bad about the recent decisions he'd made. First trusting Conrad, and then taking Billy to Hannah's. He should have known something was wrong when he saw the neighborhood where Hannah had her house. It made perfect sense once you found out she was training all of her boys to be thieves.

He decided to go to his room to wait for Roper there. When he reached his door, he hesitated. There was a scent in the air, one he thought he recognized. He didn't know what it was, but he had smelled it before, and recently.

Drawing his gun, he unlocked his door as silently as possible, then opened it quickly and sprang into the room.

Angel was so startled she gave a little scream and came out of the chair she'd been sitting in.

"Angel?"

"You . . . you frightened me!" she said, accusingly.

Now he knew what the smell was—her. She had a distinctive aroma, which he'd first noticed at the house, although he hadn't dwelled on it at the time.

"What are you doing here?" he asked, holstering his gun. "Did Hannah send you?"

"She has no idea I'm here," the girl said. "Can you close the door? I don't want anyone to see us."

Clint closed the door, then turned to face her again.

He was struck again by how beautiful she was, but something was different. She was dressed differently, decidedly older, and suddenly she looked older.

"What's different about you?" he asked.

"Oh, that," she said, with a smile. "I'm not trying to look younger. Hannah likes everyone to think I'm about fourteen."

"And how old are you?"

"Almost twenty-one," she said. "Pretty soon, I won't be able to look fourteen and Hannah won't have any use for me. That's why I need your help."

"My help? To do what?"

"To get away from her."

"Angel," he said, "I'd like to help, but—"

"Billy's in danger."

"What?"

"I heard her and the lieutenant talking," she said. "They want to get rid of you and of him."

"You mean they'd kill him?"

"I think so."

"But he's just a boy."

"They're all boys, Mr. Adams."

"Angel, I heard things about Hannah, that she trains the boys to steal? Is it true?"

"Yes," she said, "and to tell you the truth, I don't think she could get Billy to do it."

"Do you think he's in any immediate danger?"

"I don't think he's in real danger until they take care of you."

"Well," Clint said, "they had their one and only shot at me today."

"W-what happened?"

He told her about the shooting and about pursuing the shooter.

"What are you going to do?"

"I'm going to get Billy out of there."

"I can help," she said, anxious, "but you have to take me, too."

"Angel, I can't—"

"Please," she said, coming closer to him. Her scent was strong now, and heady. She pressed herself against him and he could see—and feel—that she was certainly not a fourteen-year-old girl. Her breasts were small, but they were as firm as peaches. When she was in Hannah's house she probably has them bound, but now they were unfettered and he could even feel the nipples pressing into his chest. He didn't know how she accomplished it, but she had even managed to look shorter at Hannah's house.

"Please," she said, rubbing herself against him, sliding her hand down over his crotch so that she could feel the bulge there, which he had no control over.

"Ooh," she said, unbuttoning his trousers.

"Angel, don't—"

"I'm not allowed to do anything in the house," she said, sliding her hand inside his pants and underwear. She took his penis in her hand and drew it out. "Hannah, she and the lieutenant, they do it in her office and sometimes in her bedroom. I listen, and it makes me . . . excited, but I can't do anything there."

"Angel—"

"Oooh," she said again, enjoying how hot he was in her hand. How firm and heavy he felt. "I see them, sometimes," she said. "She takes him in her mouth, like this."

Suddenly he was in her mouth. He reached down to hold her head, meaning to draw her away, but was unable to. He knew she was twenty, but she had looked fourteen at Hannah's, and although she didn't look fourteen now, neither did she look twenty.

"Mmmm," she said, sliding his dick in and out of her mouth experimentally. "I've never done this before. Is this all right?"

She took him in her mouth again and sucked on him, and suddenly he gripped her head and pulled himself free. He backed away from her and tucked himself back into his pants. From her knees she stared up at him, puzzled.

"Was I doing it wrong?" she asked.

"You were doing fine, Angel," he said, "but you don't have to do that to get me to help you."

"But, I want to—"

"If you help me get Billy out, I'll get you out as well."

"Really?"

"Yes?"

"You promise?"

"I swear."

"Oh, thank you."

She got to her feet and flung herself at him. She hugged him, and it was a childlike hug, nothing like she'd been doing moments before. However, her body was still pressed against his, and he was still reacting to her.

"Angel," he said, pushing her away.

"But can't we—"

"Maybe another time," he said, "but I'm waiting for someone right now."

"A woman?"

"No," he said. "A man, a friend who is going to help me get Billy out—and you."

"But we can—"

"Why don't you just sit?" he said, taking her by the shoulders and pushing her into a chair. Damn her, what was that scent? He felt as if he were going to burst from his pants.

"I'm going to wash my face," he told her, going into the other room, "with cold water!"

# THIRTY-SEVEN

When Talbot Roper arrived, he was surprised to see Angel sitting in a chair, hands primly in her lap.

"What's she doing here?" he asked.

"You know who she is?" Clint asked.

"Of course I do," Roper said. "That's Angel, Hannah's . . . girl."

"She wants to help us get Billy out of the house."

"In exchange for what?" Roper asked, suspiciously.

"In exchange for getting her out, too."

Roper looked at the girl dubiously.

"I know who you are, too, Mr. Roper," she said.

"What's different about her?" Roper asked Clint.

"She looks older."

Roper snapped his fingers. "That's it. How old is she?"

"Twenty," Clint said. "She says."

"Almost twenty-one," Angel added.

Clint could see that, although his friend was suspicious of the girl, he also couldn't keep his eyes off her. Also, from the flaring of his nostrils, Clint knew that

Roper smelled what he had smelled—and surmised what all men did. When Angel got even a little older, she was going to be very, very dangerous.

But that would be some other man's problem.

"We had some commotion here this morning," Clint said, turning the attention away from the girl.

"What kind of commotion?"

Clint explained about Conrad's visit, the shooting by Steve Harker, and then Conrad's killing of the man.

"He set you up," Roper said, when Clint had finished.

"I know."

"And then killed Harker so he couldn't give him away."

"Exactly."

Roper stroked his chin.

"He knows you're going after the boy?"

"I'm sure it won't come as a surprise."

"Then it won't be so easy," Roper said. "They'll be waiting for you."

"That's where it would help to have someone on the inside," Clint said.

Both men looked at Angel, who simply smiled.

"You botched it?" Hannah demanded accusingly.

"I didn't botch it," Conrad said. "That idiot Harker did."

"And who gave the job to Harker?"

Conrad hesitated, took a deep breath, let it out slowly, and said, "There's no point in assigning blame now, Hannah. We have to decide what will happen next."

"What will happen," Hannah said, patiently, "is that Adams will come for the boy."

"Then we'll have to be ready for him."

"Yes, we will." Hannah fell silent for a moment, then exploded. "God! I should kill that stupid woman!"

"What woman?"

"Sandy," Hannah said. "For sending Adams here. Oh, never mind now. Do you have some men you can bring over here?"

"I can get them," Conrad said.

"Then do it," Hannah said. "Get them over here as quickly as possible. We have to be ready whenever he comes."

"What about the boy?"

"We don't touch the boy until after we've taken care of Adams," Hannah said. "The boy is our bait."

"Right."

As Conrad turned to leave, Hannah said, "Robert?"

"Yeah?"

"We can't afford another mistake."

"I know."

Hannah put both of her fists on her desk, leaned on them, and said very pointedly, "Then . . . don't . . . let . . . it . . . happen . . . again!"

After Conrad had left, Hannah sat back in her chair and thought about the boy, Billy. She had spent some time with him that day and was impressed with his intelligence. He was smarter than boys two or three years older than he was, and she could see that he would be a fast learner. The only problem with him was that he seemed to be uncompromisingly honest. That could turn out be a big problem when you wanted to teach a boy to steal.

Still, there was a possibility that, with Clint Adams out of the way, she could take the time to work on Billy and make him her greatest student. Her secret weapon would be, as it had been in the past with so many boys, Angel.

But where had that stupid girl gotten to?

# THIRTY-EIGHT

Clint and Roper finally came up with a plan while Angel sat there and listened. It occurred to Clint that the girl could very well go back to Hannah and tell her everything, but he decided to trust his instincts with her, and they told him that she really did want to get away from Hannah. Granted, his instincts hadn't been very good when it came to Lieutenant Conrad or to Hannah herself, but he put that down to his concern with getting Billy someplace safe.

They were all seated in the hotel room now, and Roper noticed Clint rubbing his injured leg.

"How's that leg doing?"

Clint looked down because he hadn't noticed that he was rubbing it. He wondered how long he'd been doing it.

His first thought was to lie, but he and Roper would be watching each other's back later.

"It hurts."

"Let's have a look."

Clint started to pull his pant leg up but then decided

to simply pull the pants down. Angel wasn't going to see anything she hadn't seen earlier.

"You need a new bandage," Roper said.

"I can do it," Angel said.

Roper looked at her.

"Have you done it before?"

"Yes, many times."

Roper looked at Clint.

"It's fine with me."

"Can you get me the water and bandages?" she asked Roper.

"Sure."

She got up from her chair, knelt in front of Clint, and began undoing the bloody bandage.

"Thank you, Angel."

Without looking at him she said, "That's not really my name, you know. It's a name Hannah gave me."

"What's your real name?"

She made a face and said, "Gertrude."

"Do you want me to call you Gertrude?"

"No!" she snapped. "I hate that name."

"What would you like to be called?"

"I wanted to be called Angela," she said, "but Hannah said I was too young to pick my own name, so she called me Angel."

"So what should I call you?"

She sighed.

"Call me Angel," she said, finally. "It's what I've been called since I was ten."

"You've been with Hannah that long?"

"Yes."

"Why do you want to leave, then?"

"She treats the boys better than me," Angel said. "She

always treats me like a servant, makes me tuck the boys in and kiss them good night."

"Do you like the boys?"

"No," she said. "They're nasty. They always have been, and the older I get the nastier they seem. Except for Billy. He seems to be a really nice boy."

"He is."

"You have to get him away before she kills him," Angel said, "or worse."

"What could be worse?"

She finished unwrapping his wound and looked up at him.

"She could decide to keep him and make him one of her boys," she said. "For a boy like Billy, *that* would be worse."

# THIRTY-NINE

While Angel cleaned the wound and rebandaged the leg, Roper asked Clint if he wanted him to bring in some help.

"I don't think so," Clint said. "I think the two of us can handle it quietly."

"Or noisily, if it comes to that," Roper said. "Angel, does Hannah have any men in the house?"

"No," Angel said, "only the policeman, Lieutenant Conrad."

"Conrad will bring in some men," Clint said. "Do you have any idea who he'd use, Tal?"

"I might figure it out, given time," Roper said, "but I'm assuming you want to go in tonight?"

"Today," Clint said.

"In daylight?" Roper asked. "I assumed you'd want to use the cover of night."

"They'll probably assume that, too," Clint said. "Let's cross them up. Let's go in in broad daylight."

"And I guess you want to use the front door, too?" Roper asked.

"No," Clint said, "the back door will do. Angel will open it for us."

"I'll go back right away," she said. "Hannah will probably be looking for me."

"Where will you tell her you went?" Clint asked.

"I'll buy something on the way home, and she'll think that's what I went out for."

"Let me give you some money—" Clint started, but she stopped him.

"No," she said. "I save the money she gives me to buy myself little things. If I spend too much she'll get suspicious."

"Smart girl," Roper said.

Angel wrapped Clint's leg and made it tight, then sat back on her heels and looked at him.

"You will take me out of there, too, won't you?" she asked.

"I said I would, didn't I?"

"I've been lied to before," she said.

"He's not lying," Roper said, "and neither am I. But you better not be lying either, Angel."

"I'm not."

"Then we're all telling the truth," Clint said. "Let's get this done today. Angel, how long will it take you to get back to the house?"

"About an hour," she said. "To be safe you better give me two. Hannah will probably scold me for a while and give me some jobs to do around the house. It will take me some time to get the back door unlocked."

"Well," Roper said, "while you're doing your chores, see if you can check out how many men Conrad puts in the house and where they are."

"I will," Angel said.

"And be careful, Angel," Clint said. "Don't do anything that's going to make Hannah suspicious of you."

"Don't worry," she said, getting to her feet. "I'm used to sneaking around that house without anybody noticing me."

Roper walked her to the door and let her out, then returned to Clint as he was testing out his leg.

"You gonna be all right?" Roper asked.

"I'll be fine," Clint said. "What's a little soreness? It'll keep me alert."

"It'll keep you cripple, if you're not careful," Roper said. "When this is over you better find someplace to light and stay for a while until you heal."

"That's good advice," Clint said, "and when this is all over, I'll take it—right after I find that boy someplace safe to stay this time."

"You're still going to have a problem if he doesn't want to leave, you know," Roper said. "We'll have to keep him quiet."

"Don't worry," Clint said. "With Angel on our side, he'll want to go, and he'll keep quiet."

"I hope you're right."

"Yeah," Clint said. He flexed his leg and said to himself, "I hope so, too."

When Angel reentered the house about an hour later, Hannah was right on her.

"Where have you been?"

Angel flinched. She knew that Hannah liked when she could scare her. In point of fact, Hannah's shouting did scare her, so there really wasn't that much acting involved.

"I just went shopp—"

"Never mind," Hannah said. "I don't care what little trinket you bought for yourself this time. I keep telling you to save your money, but do you listen to me? You keep wasting it. That's up to you. I've got some chores for you to do."

"Yes, ma'am."

"And listen good," Hannah said, "because I'm only going to tell you once."

"Yes, ma'am."

"There'll be some men in the house today," Hannah said, "so this is what I want you to do. . . ."

# FORTY

"How many men have you got in my house?" Hannah asked Conrad. She had left Angel to her chores and gone into her office, where Conrad was waiting.

"Three."

"Is that enough for Adams?" she asked, sitting behind her desk.

"Three, and me," he added.

She opened her top drawer, took out a gun, set it on the desk, and said, "Don't forget me."

"See?" he said. "We have plenty of help."

"I hope you're right," she said. "I don't want anything messing us up, Robert. We have a good thing going here."

" 'We,' Hannah?" he asked.

"Of course, 'we.' What do you think?"

"Well," he said, "you're making it sound like we're partners and not like I'm just on your payroll."

She looked at him and bit her lip. It was the first time he had ever seen her unsure,

"Well . . . maybe you aren't just on my payroll."

"What are you saying, Hannah?"

She bit her lip harder, then shook her head.

"Nothing," she answered, "I'm not saying anything . . . yet. Let's see what happens when this Adams thing is over."

Conrad had the feeling that all he had to do was kill Clint Adams, and Hannah Smith would be his.

That was all the incentive he needed.

"Where are you going?" she asked, as he got up and headed for the door.

"I'm going to check on the men," he said. "I want to make damned *sure* this doesn't get messed up."

He went out the door, and she smiled. It was amazing what you could get a man to do just by biting your lip.

It took Angel almost the full two hours before she was able to find her way to the back door, and then there was a man standing there. She retreated before he could see her and went to the kitchen to get a cup of coffee.

"I thought you might like this," she said as she approached the man. He was in his twenties, and she could see immediately that he was susceptible to her charms, even though she was once again dressed like she was fourteen.

"Thank you, ma'am," he said, accepting the coffee.

"Do you have to stay in this hallway all the time?" she asked him.

"Well, uh, no, ma'am," the man said. "I'm just sort of supposed to move around—ya know, keep my eyes open."

"Well," she said, moving closer to him, "if you get upstairs anytime, my room's right near the top of the staircase."

She saw his nostrils flare as he caught her scent. She didn't know what it was anymore than men did, but she knew that she gave off a scent that men liked.

"Uh, you're a might young, aintcha, ma'am?" he asked.

She could see from the bulge in front of his pants that his body didn't think she was too young. She stuck one finger into his belt and tugged, then slid her hand down so that she was holding his bulge in the palm of her hand.

"I'm old enough," she said. She didn't think she'd have to go through with what she was promising, but even if she did, he was kind of cute. She stood on her toes and kissed him, taking his bottom lip between her teeth just for a moment, then releasing it and licking it, all the time keeping her hand pressed against his warm bulge. Hell, she was almost twenty-one, it was time for her to get out from under Hannah's thumb in more ways than one.

"Just think about it," she whispered.

"Um, I w-will," he said.

"And if you're finished in this hall," she said, "I got to clean it."

"Yes, ma'am," he said. "I'm finished."

"Take the coffee cup with you and just put it down anywhere when you're done," she said. "I'll pick it up later."

"Y-yes, ma'am."

He went off down the hall, walking the way she knew men walked when their crotch was full, and then he disappeared around the corner. Immediately she went to the back door and unlocked it.

Now she had to find Billy.

• • •

Clint and Roper had worked their way around to the back of the house and heard the click of the lock when Angel turned it.

"That's it," Clint said. "We're in."

Roper was frowning.

"What's wrong?"

"Why wouldn't they have anyone outside the house?" he wondered, aloud.

"Maybe they want us to come inside," Clint said.

"And we're gonna oblige them, ain't we?"

"Yes," Clint said, turning the doorknob, "we are."

# FORTY-ONE

When they were inside, in the rear hall, Clint said to Roper, "We want the boy, and then we want to get out."

"And after that?" Roper's tone matched Clint's, quiet and hushed.

"I don't care," Clint said. "I don't care if Hannah goes on doing what she's doing with Conrad as her partner, I just want the boy out. I'll take him someplace else and find him a home."

"I don't think Hannah and Conrad will see it that way."

"I don't care," Clint said. "I'll check upstairs, you check down. We'll meet back here."

"Never mind that," Roper said. "You find that boy, you get him out. Don't worry about me."

"The girl comes, too," Clint reminded him.

"I remember."

"First sound of a shot," Clint said, "all bets are off. If you've got the boy, the girl, whatever, you get them out."

"We're all getting out together," Roper said.

"Okay."

Clint went in one direction, Roper in the other.

Around the corner, Clint found a stairway leading up. He started up, stopped when one step creaked, then continued up until he reached the second floor. Just as he made it to the top landing a man appeared carrying a coffee cup.

"What th—" the man said. He dropped the coffee cup and went for his gun. Clint reached out, grabbed a handful of the man's shirt, stepped aside, and pulled. When he released the shirt, the man went careening down the stairway, his gun still in his holster. When he hit the bottom he just laid there, not moving. Clint had no time to check to se if he was alive or dead. Someone might have heard the commotion.

He started down the second-floor hall.

Angel found Billy in the third-floor room he shared with three other boys. Only these four boys were left in the house. The others were out doing what Hannah had taught them, stealing and picking pockets, and bringing the proceeds back to her. These three boys were supposed to keep Billy company until Hannah got around to him.

None of these boys had talked to Billy about stealing. That was Hannah's job. However, they had all talked about Angel, and when she entered they all blushed.

"Come on, Billy."

"Where to?" he asked.

"Hannah wants you."

Billy stood up and said, "I'll see you guys later."

They all nodded, looking at each other, but not at Angel.

"You boys all stay in your room until I come for you," she said. "Got it?"

"We got it," the older boy said. He was all of eleven.

"Come on, Billy," she said, taking his hand and leading him from the room.

In the hall he asked, "What does Hannah want?"

"It's not Hannah who wants you," Angel said to him, "it's Clint."

"What's Clint want?"

"To take us away from here?"

"What? But I don't wanna—"

Angel turned and knelt down in front of Billy so she could look into his eyes.

"Billy, do you trust me?"

"Y-yes, but—"

"This is a bad place, Billy," she said. "Clint didn't know it when he left you here, but he does now, and he's coming to get you."

"Why is it a bad place?"

"Just take my word for it," she said, "it is. We have to get out of here."

"You're coming, too?" the boy asked.

"Yes," she said, "I'm coming, too."

That seemed to satisfy the boy.

"Okay, let's go."

She nodded, stood, grabbed his hand, and turned to leave, but standing in her way was Lieutenant Conrad.

"What's this?"

Angel was at a loss for words, staring at the policeman.

"Clint's gonna get us out," Billy said to Conrad.

The policeman looked at him, smiled, and said, "Is that right, little man?"

Billy nodded and said, "Angel says so."

"She does, does she?"

Angel closed her eyes.

# FORTY-TWO

Clint found the second floor empty and then discovered the stairway to a third floor. He was about to start up when he heard footsteps from down the hall. He retreated to one of the empty rooms and closed the door, leaving it ajar so he could look out. What he saw was Lieutenant Conrad turn a corner and come down the hall. The man didn't seem to be in a hurry, so he must not have seen the unconscious man at the foot of the back stairs. Once that man was discovered there'd be an alarm raised, for sure.

As he watched, Conrad started to go past the stairs to the third floor, then stopped, looked up, and then started up. There was no way Clint could go up now that Conrad was up there. He was just going to have to wait.

Then he heard Conrad say, "What's this?"

He left the room and hurried to the foot of the stairs in time to hear the policeman say, "Is that right, little man?"

He started up the steps when he heard a voice behind him say, "Who the hell are you?"

• • •

After leaving Clint in the back hall, Roper found another hallway and followed it. It led him to the front of the house, which he imagined was so large it must be like a maze. He wondered how many men Conrad would have figured he'd need?

He was moving past a doorway when he heard voices inside, a man and a woman. He stopped to listen.

Hannah Wells had come to a decision. She decided that when this was all over she was going to have to come to a parting of the ways with Conrad. He'd been making too many mistakes lately, and she'd only been keeping him around for sex. However, she'd also decided that she needed a younger man for that. When the lieutenant brought in the three men he was going to use this afternoon, one of them caught her eye; a big, strapping, handsome man in his thirties, roughly ten years younger than she was. As Conrad introduced them to her she retained only that man's name, Saunders. She decided there and then to "try" him out, at the same time letting him know who he was working for.

She was in her office, sitting at her desk, when someone stopped in the doorway. She looked up and saw Saunders looking at her. The way he was looking at her gave her the chills.

"Are you all right, ma'am?" he asked.

"I'm fine."

"Mr. Conrad said we was to check every room," he said. "I didn't know this was your office."

"Your name is Saunders, isn't it?"

"That's right."

She stood up.

"What's your first name?"

"Bill."

"Why don't you come in, Bill?" she asked. "I'd like to talk to you."

By the time Roper came to Hannah's office door, she and Saunders had gone past the talking stage. He put his ear to the door and listened.

"Ma'am," he heard a man say, "I'm supposed to be patrolling the house."

"The lieutenant and those other two can handle it for the moment, Bill—oh, my, you're a big one, aren't you?"

"Uh, ma'am—"

"Don't you like women, Bill?"

"Uh, yes, ma'am—"

"Oooh, I can see you like me. It's getting bigger."

"Jesus—" Roper heard the man say.

Just then there was a shot from another part of the house. Roper reacted immediately, opening the door and stepping in with his gun drawn.

Hannah was on her knees in front of a man whose trousers were around his ankles. She'd obviously had his erect penis in her mouth, and, as she whipped her head around in surprise, her teeth must have caught him because he yelled, "Ow! Shit!"

Even though he was in pain, the man started to reach for his gun. Unfortunately it was down around his ankles with his pants. But it was where Hannah could reach it, and she went for it immediately.

"Don't!" Roper shouted, but it didn't do any good.

• • •

Clint turned and saw the man coming toward him, his gun not drawn yet.

"I said, who the hell—hey, you're him!"

The man went for his gun. Clint swore aloud, drew and shot him dead center in the chest, and he knew all hell was about to break loose.

# FORTY-THREE

Clint didn't wait for the man to hit the floor. He turned to run up the stairs, but Lieutenant Conrad was already coming down. He had his gun in one hand, and Billy under his other arm. The gun was pointing at the boy. Clint couldn't see Angel anywhere.

"Back off, Adams!" Conrad said. "I'll put a bullet in the boy's head."

Clint backed down until he was off the staircase. He was wearing his regular holster for this excursion to liberate Billy from Hannah's clutches, but he also still had the New Line tucked into his belt at the small of his back.

"Drop the gun."

Clint let his Colt drop to the floor.

"Kick it down the hall."

Clint did as he was told.

"Where's Angel?" Clint asked.

"He hit her with his gun!" Billy said, outraged. "She was bleeding."

"Keep still and quiet," Conrad told the boy.

"Do as he says, Billy."

Billy fell quiet and remained still.

"You people," Clint said, shaking his head. "You and Hannah, all you had to do was turn us away."

"Hannah thought that would be suspicious since her friend Sandy sent you."

"And Sandy? Does she know what her friend does with her boys?" Clint asked.

"Not a clue," Conrad said. "That's why she sent you. She thought Hannah's place was a legitimate home for boys."

"Well, what do we do now, Lieutenant?" Clint asked.

"Well, I can't very well let you walk out of here alive, can I, Adams?" Conrad said. "I mean, there'd go my career."

"I didn't come alone."

"Who'd you—Roper? He came with you? I've got three other men in the house."

"Well, one of them is lying at the foot of the back stairs, and I heard shots from downstairs, so I'd bet that another one is down. And since I just shot the third one, I'm going to concern myself solely with you."

Conrad still had not reached the bottom of the steps, but he took the gun away from Billy's head and pointed it at Clint. That's what Clint had been waiting for and, apparently, Angel as well.

Clint couldn't see her, but the girl had dragged herself, bleeding from a gash in her forehead, to the top of the stairs. Now that Conrad had removed the gun from Billy's head, she threw herself down the stairs at Conrad like a human cannonball. She struck him in the small of the back, and he and Billy both went flying down the remaining steps along with her.

They all sprawled onto the floor and, amazingly enough, Conrad held on to his gun—which was too bad.

Clint pulled the New Line from behind him. Conrad tried to grab for the boy, but Billy skittered away from him, so the detective looked at Clint and started to bring the gun around,.

"Don't!" Clint said, but it was too late. There was no stopping Conrad, and Clint had no choice.

Clint came down the front stairs with Billy and Angel and found Roper waiting in the front hall. Angel was holding one hand over her cut head and had had her other arm around Billy.

"Hannah?" Clint asked as they reached the bottom of the stairs.

"She picked the wrong time to audition a new man in her life," Roper said.

"She's dead?" Angel asked.

"Yes," Roper said. "I'm sorry."

"I'm not."

"Conrad said he had others—"

"Mmm," Roper said. "They're gone. I let the one I found her with go. He's gonna need a doctor for a, uh, delicate part of his body. With Hannah dead, he had no reason to stick around. After all, she was paying the bills."

"I left one at the foot of the back stairs."

"Dead," Roper said. "Broken neck."

"So the house is clean?"

"Just us and the mice."

"Oh," Angel said, "there are three boys upstairs waiting for me. I'll get them."

"I'll come with you!" Billy said, and they both ran back up.

"Is it safe?" Roper asked.

"Like you said," Clint answered. "Just us and the mice."

"Conrad?"

"Dead."

"So what now?" Roper asked. "What about the boy?"

"I'm wondering," Clint said, "if the city might have somebody who could take this place over."

"There are lots of little thieves living here," Roper said.

"They learned how to steal," Clint said, "they can learn how not to."

"Maybe they can," Roper said. "How's the leg?"

"Sore."

"You're going to need some rest."

"I'll take it."

"Oh," Roper said, "while we're waiting, I might as well tell you that I got a line on your friend Sandy's husband and son. Looks like they're in Chicago."

"When did you find that out?"

"Yesterday evening."

"And you're just telling me now?"

"Well," Roper said with a helpless shrug, "in all the excitement, I guess I just forgot."